The Black Arrows:

Succession Secured

Mark Budd

With Eternal Gratitude:

For the guidance and support of my editor
Helen Bethune Moore

And for the patience of my wife
Narrissa Leanne Budd

Without both of you this would not have been possible.

TABLE OF CONTENTS

PROLOGUE

—— ✦ ——

Impatient hooves pawed the ground. Reins were held firmly in check. The vast column of cavalry and troopers stood in place – waiting. A stiff westerly breeze chilled their faces as if warding them away from the invisible line that marked the border.

All eyes focussed on the silhouetted figure who sat astride his horse, overlooking them from a slight rise, beneath a flag of his unfurled colours. Duke Jacoby could sense the movement and feel the wind pulling on his cloak. The breeze was of no significance to him. His mind was set.

A grin tugged at the corner of the Duke's lips. That he had been able to amass his army of regulars and mercenaries in secret evidenced his superiority as a statesman and a general.

His cause was just.

For years, the Duke had been undermining the reign of King Alfred the First. His people had sabotaged trade negotiations with other kingdoms, paid bandits to take what was not theirs, and whispered words of dissent and dissatisfaction with the King's rule wherever they might bear fruit.

The Duke was satisfied that his covert action had weakened his brother's grip on the crown. He had bided his time within his tangled web. Now was the time to act – decisively and surgically. He would seize the opportunity to speed his accession to the throne. His knowledge was his power. His source, from within the King's inner circle, was impeccable.

It was time for the Duke to advance his place in the line of succession, in a manner that would prove the doubters of his prowess to be wrong, and for his supporters to be emboldened. He could almost feel the weight of the crown being lowered upon his head.

Drawing his sword from its jewel-encrusted scabbard, the Duke paused to appreciate the light reflecting from the rubies in its pommel before he raised the weapon high above his head and gestured for his troops to move forward. A cheer rose from his men as the long column began to flow over the border and into Baron Aethelson's land.

The Duke watched his army move, secure in the knowledge that its route had been carefully planned from information received from the squads of his elite scouts who had long since preceded it. Nothing had been left to chance; success, he reflected, was certain. He had waited long enough. Patience could, and should, be set aside.

The Duke nudged his horse forward. His brother's troops were not there to prevent his crossing. The element of surprise was his. The speed of his advance would catch out the King's allies. He had played his brother's options over in his head and with his advisors; there was no counter. The isolated location, the resources available to the Baron and the King's position were all known and accounted for. Once he was successful in his endeavour, his supporters could shrug off the cloak of their anonymity and flock to his side; with their support, he would seize the crown.

It was time for the Duke to secure his destiny. It was time for the Duke to become king.

ONE

As the echoes of the fight subsided, the grim spectacle became apparent. Sixteen men and one boy had been on a routine patrol for Baron Aethelson. They had been following a narrow country road between the fields of the district's farmers when they had decided to cross a meandering creek and tramp through a field of wheat. They had intended to take a break beneath the imposing limbs of a vast, solitary oak tree. As they walked, they'd chuckled at lewd jokes, whose subject matter had been drawn from their long experience together.

It was only because of his mother's stubborn insistence that Barney had accompanied his father's patrol. Her final words to him had been blunt and harsh, but he had come to understand that, in her own way, she had been trying to prepare him for what she saw as the inevitability of his future.

He recalled what she had said. He had been playing her statement over and over in his head for most of the time that he had spent with the patrol. "You have been taught to read so that you can serve. You'll never amount to anything more than a guard on the Baron's battlements. You'll be on the outside looking in at your master in his well-lit and warm hall, not on the inside looking out. It's not such a bad life. Your father is testament to that. He enjoys the camaraderie and the simplicity. You'll get used to it once you've stopped dreaming. You need to accept your destiny."

Despite his mother's well-meant intentions and the fact that he could find no fault in her reasoning, Barney thirsted for knowledge. He wanted to challenge his mother's belief that his fate was sealed, not because he was rebellious, but because he was troubled by the notion that he was not free to make his own choices. He did not see why he was predestined to walk the same path as his father. As the patrol walked, Barney used his fingers to roll a pawn from his father's chess set around in his pocket. He wondered why the tactics of that game so soothed him.

Barney had moved away from his father's side, towards the trunk of the vast oak tree. He had decided to climb it so that he could feel the breeze in his hair and take in the view.

No one from the patrol saw the empty encampment until they stumbled into it. At the patrol's approach there was no call to arms. Unusually, the men-at-arms had made no attempt to run. Once alerted, the camp's soldiers had all withdrawn quickly and quietly into the surrounding foliage.

The first arrow entered Barney's father's throat with such speed and with such force that it didn't stop moving until the black feathers of its flight had become entangled with the flesh of the arrow's entry point. The arrow's black shaft was buried so deep that the arrowhead had exited out through the nape of his neck, carrying with it the deadly barbed tip.

For a brief moment, the patrol didn't react. It was almost as if it was frozen in place. No swords were drawn, and no shields were raised. In that moment the patrol lost the skirmish.

From the onset of the attack Barney was ignored. He had no weapon and was too young to be a threat. He was merely a spectator to events that he was powerless to influence.

Because Barney had been making a beeline to the tree, he was to one side of the main group that, in seconds, was filled with broken and dying men. He watched the final stand of the survivors with disbelief. They came together with raised shields and drawn swords, but through their initial surprise and hesitation they had lost the initiative, and without any suggestion of a parlay by the aggressors, they must have known that they were going to die.

Barney didn't know what to do. As the last of the Baron's men fell, the dying man caught sight of Barney and shouted at him to flee.

Barney turned and ran! He never saw the man who had warned him crumple to the ground. Barney was the only survivor and therefore the only witness to the events. Despite having never been fast on his feet, he reacted with just enough speed that an arrow aimed at him passed harmlessly behind him. At least one of the Duke's men had seen him. And one was enough. He was sure to alert the rest of the Duke's scouts.

As tears streamed down his face and panic lent him speed, Barney put his head down and raced into the field of wheat, which swallowed him in its embrace, giving no second chance to the now unsighted archer.

Barney was both protected and confused by the tall golden stalks of wheat. He had no idea in which direction he was running, but he quickly realised that he couldn't be seen by his pursuers, and he couldn't hear the feverish baying of any hunting dogs. He just might have the advantage. Any sounds that he heard, above the rustling of the wheat, could only come from the ambushers.

With difficulty, Barney drew back from his panicked flight and jogged. He slowed his breathing to control his panting and thus reduce the envelope of noise that surrounded him. Eventually, his ears were cleared of the pounding of his own heartbeat and he was able to listen for sounds of pursuit. When he heard something, he moved in the opposite direction as quickly and as silently as possible, the wheat shifting around him like rippling water. As the wind strengthened, it lent his movement further cover while carrying the sounds of pursuit clearly to him.

The leader of the ambush was distressed. His orders had been to leave no witnesses alive while he scouted the area for the most direct and secretive route to the Baron's castle. Now he was worried. He was not particularly well liked, and his second-in-command coveted his position. The man would think nothing of exposing his failure to the Duke. He could hear his accuser pointing out that a young lad, who had less capacity for intelligent thought than a lowly peasant, had evaded him. He would be scorned and lucky to keep his command. If only he had been permitted to bring his dogs.

Alas, they had been kept with the wagon train that supported the Duke's main force so as not to unwittingly alert the enemy.

"Bring up the horses. Send six men ahead to circle to the stream on the far side of the field. The rest of you, mount up and spread out. As we advance, make some noise, keep your eyes open and drive the boy before you."

In quick time the plan was put into action. Barney could clearly hear the party as it advanced. He jogged away from the jingling of the bridles and the snorting of the horses. He felt confident that he would remain unseen until he realised that his pursuers would now have a definite height advantage from their horses. Understanding led to fear, and fear motivated him to run.

As he ran, he kept looking over his shoulder. Barney was so preoccupied with what he was fleeing from that he didn't notice an overgrown drainage ditch. His left foot stepped into space. Pain shot up from his ankle and his lower back as his foot found the bottom of the ditch where it caught, causing him to pitch forward. Barney let out a cry of pain and surprise before his face slammed into the ground, knocking him senseless.

The Duke's scouts were relieved to hear their quarry. Those following fanned out their horses and spurred them towards the source of the sound. Their six compatriots, who had moved to the stream, changed their position so that they were, once more, directly opposite to where they thought the boy was. When they were confident that they were best placed to prevent the boy's escape, they stopped.

Barney's senses came back to him quickly, but their return brought pain. Putting the knuckle of his right index finger into his mouth, he bit down hard so that he did not cry out, while mentally he worked hard to reduce the pain of his ankle to a background sensory noise. He could now clearly hear the riders urging their mounts on.

The ditch was barely broad enough for Barney to lie on his belly. It stank. The mud oozed around him as he slid into it and pulled his way along it. Momentarily, he considered that his mother would be mad at him for ruining his clothes, but he stayed down. He would deal with the consequences of his action later. With his nose nearly touching the fetid water, he half crawled, half slithered along.

Frustratingly, even though the wind had begun to die down, the cavalry could neither hear nor see any sign of their quarry. From their vantage point, they should have been able to see bending stalks of wheat but there was no evidence of his passage. This was bad. Had the boy guessed that they were driving him into danger? Had he gone to ground? Had they passed him?

The scouts became increasingly frantic. Heads rapidly turned and their horses, sensing their riders' flight-and-fight response to no apparent danger, became harder to control. Gradually, the tight line-abreast cordon began to break down.

Barney could hear the breathing of the closest horses. He knew that unless the riders turned away, they would find the ditch and unless they were stupid, they would know where to look for him. His ankle was now swollen to double its normal size, so even if he had wanted to, he couldn't run. The ditch was his only cover.

Turning flat on his back Barney pressed himself down so that only his nose and mouth remained above the water. Grasping handfuls of mud, wheat and weeds, he placed them haphazardly along his body to try to camouflage his position.

Without fanfare, a second group of horsemen entered the field at a trot and approached the scouts. A shouted greeting was followed by a brief explanation of events. More shouting. Orders this time.

The men nearest Barney, together with those waiting for him on the far side of the field, now walked their mounts to converge with the newcomers. The Duke's army was on the move, and it was speed rather than stealth that they now aimed for. Whether the boy escaped was now largely irrelevant.

Barney could hear nothing. His ears were full of water and mud. As the cold leached into his skin, he found it increasingly difficult to lie still. The stench made his eyes water and his nose run. He lay directly between the merging cavalry.

As the cavalry came together they discovered the muddy ditch. One of the riders signalled quietly to another and the two of them stopped their horses and dismounted.

It was simple for the men to follow Barney's tracks. When they came to where the tracks ended, they could pick out the outline of the boy in the mud. The marks he had made, when he had dragged himself through the mud, pointed to his position as clearly as if someone had drawn an arrow.

Gesturing to his compatriot, one of the scouts moved around behind Barney's head and the other drew a short knife.

The first Barney knew that he had been spotted was when he was grasped by the hair and pulled from the ditch. Struggling, he reached for the hand that held him.

Barney's slimy hair and the stickiness of the mud in the ditch saved him. As the second man lunged forward with his dagger to strike Barney through his heart, Barney started slipping from his captor's grasp. As Barney slid, the knife missed its intended target and plunged into the soft tissue between his shoulder and his heart. By sheer luck, the wound was not instantly fatal; however, gushing blood was evidence enough that a mortal wound had, most likely, been struck.

The pain caused Barney to pass out. His deadweight was reason enough for his captor to lose purchase on Barney's hair. Barney's body slithered away from the hand that held him. The man shook the mud from his fingers and spat at the boy's apparently lifeless form as it slid further down into the drain. Useless peasants, he thought, they breed like cockroaches and infest the land.

Both of the scouts believed that the knife had pierced the boy's heart. Not wanting more mud to spatter their tunics, they left Barney to his fate. In response to their commander's orders, they remounted and urged their horses towards the others. They were off to war; there were bigger prizes to capture.

Even now, in his semi-conscious state, Barney could feel the disappointment of his parents. When he died, he would not be able to serve the Baron as a guard.

———— ✦ ————

Farmer Tom had noticed the Baron's patrol from one of his many fields. It was unusual for a patrol to be in the area, so he had followed it from afar to ensure that it left his land. He had been distressed when the patrol had left the road which led around his fields to stomp through his crop towards the large oak tree that had been planted by his great-great-grandfather. He was even more distressed and startled by the ambush. When the first arrow flew, he had thrown himself to the ground despite knowing that he was too far away for any of the armed men to have seen him.

Although his view of the skirmish was partially obscured, from where he lay, Farmer Tom could see that after the victors mounted their horses they had spread out so that they could search his crop for someone or something.

The arrival of the second party of well-armed cavalry concerned him, but when they all rode off, he felt that it was safe to rise. He knew that there were dead men in the grass at the base of the tree. Grunting to himself, he turned around and strode back towards his homestead. Waste not, want not, he thought. There would be new boots for him and Maggie as well as good steel that he could use to repair his farm.

Barney half woke. Excruciating pain enveloped him. He fell back into darkness's embrace.

Some two hours later Farmer Tom returned with his cart, his wife Maggie and his two daughters, Shine and Lucy. He carried with him a long knife that would have been better used for clearing weeds than defending against the sword of a skilled opponent.

"Shine, approach Granda's tree from the right; Lucy from the left. I'll take the middle. Maggie, you come up with the cart when I signal. Don't let Bitza off her leash. Don't look at the dead folk. Look at the horizon. Call out if ya see any movement and then take to the fields and run for home."

The three crept towards the lonely tree. With every step, they cautiously watched for movement that might betray danger.

Barney shuddered. He felt cold but so hot. Once again, he passed out.

When Farmer Tom and his family arrived at the scene of the battle, they found no wounded men, only corpses, their features forever set in expressions that spoke of horror and pain, and awareness of their impending demise.

Satisfied that there was no danger, Farmer Tom gestured for Maggie to bring up the cart. Without much discussion the family gathered clothing, quivers of arrows, bows, swords and anything else that they could use at the farm.

Farmer Tom was particularly pleased to find two sets of boots that were his size and several knives that would replace his dull skinning blades. He would have to come back to bury the bodies in the morning before they were found. It was better for all evidence of the battle on his land to disappear or he was likely to be accused by the Baron of contributing to the patrol's demise. In the meantime, the sun was setting. It was time to eat.

Bitza, her tail wagging continuously, was whining in the cart. Once Farmer Tom felt that they had managed to collect everything that would be of use, he reached up and untied her.

"Come on, girl. Your turn. Quickly now. What was them men searching for? Maggie, you and the girls follow in the cart. They was looking for something down yonder. The crop is already so trampled that no harm will be done if we pass through it. Let's be seeing if Bitza can find something."

Bitza was having fun. The smells of this field, to which she rarely came, were new and exciting and there was mud for her to roll in. The joy of it! Master wasn't happy with her, but the other members of her pack were laughing.

Farmer Tom's boot connected with Bitza, propelling her on from where she had been rolling. Yelping in pain she sprang away. "Wait. A new smell. Mud. Blood. Human."

Bitza started barking.

Farmer Tom had almost caught up with his family. At first, he dismissed Bitza's barking. Then he called for her, again and again. When Bitza stoutly refused to come, Farmer Tom was both annoyed and intrigued. He made his way over to where Bitza stood. The dog bounded excitedly and proudly showed her master the man-child.

Barney awoke trembling. The water was so very cold. His left arm refused to move. His ankle was so swollen that he could not feel his toes. He vaguely heard voices, and a horse being urged on. They had come back for him. Once again, his mind switched off, but not before a vivid picture of the feathered flight of the black arrow puckering at his father's flesh teased his senses.

Farmer Tom prodded the boy with his foot. Barney didn't move.

"What is it, Tom?" yelled Maggie from the wagon.

"A boy. Dead by the looks of it."

"Is he breathing?"

"Dunno. He stinks so bad that I ain't going near him. The drainage system must be clogged. I'll be looking into it later."

Maggie slowly and carefully lowered herself down off the cart and waddled to the boy. She pressed her hand to his chest. No movement. He was dead. Sighing at the waste she leaned down harder on him, pushing to help her rise. Barney coughed involuntarily as the pressure forced air from his lungs.

"He's alive," she said. "Can we keep him?"

"We don't need another mouth to feed. Besides, he'll be dying soon."

"Now look Tom, Marcus ain't coming back from the Wall and Shine and Lucy won't ever be strong enough to do your work. Besides, if you're right and he dies soon, then we won't have to feed him anything."

"I ain't caring for him."

"Well, I ain't leaving him. No mother would do that. He wears no sword and is too young to be any sort of thug. He'll be coming home with us. As a mother of three, I say that it ain't proper to leave him here. He can choose to stay or leave when he wakes and can walk. It'll be up to him. If he stays, he'll earn his keep."

Maggie might have been short and stout, but she had actively worked the farm with her Tom for many years and so Barney's weight was insignificant to her. She lifted Barney into the back of the wagon. Tom was right. The boy stank!

"Yer a fool, Maggie. Ya don't need the extra work. It'll be up to ya and the girls."

Barney felt himself being lifted, heard voices and then, yet again, he lost all sense of reality.

THREE

Tom took hold of the reins from the driver's bench seat and motioned for Shine to join him. Shine tossed her hair to one side and climbed up alongside her father before beckoning for Bitza to join her. She and Tom both rolled their eyes as Maggie and Lucy moved the scavenged equipment aside so that they could lie Barney on the rough wooden boards of the floor of the open wagon. Once they were settled, Tom flicked the reins across the horse's back and they started towards home.

"Gently now," said Maggie to Lucy. "Let's clear the mud from his face and mouth. I'm not sure where the blood is coming from."

Maggie slowly tipped their flasks to allow water to flow in small rivulets down Barney's face and neck. When they had run out of water Maggie snapped her fingers and held out her hand towards Tom, who begrudgingly handed over his flask.

They had wiped Barney's face clean and were working on his neck when some of the water disturbed the mud that had been plugging Barney's wound. Once the mud broke away, the blood started flowing again. There was now no doubt about the wound's severity.

Lucy, seeing her mother's distress spoke quietly to her. "Ma, like you've always said, it ain't over until it's over."

Maggie was caught off guard. The knowledge of the healing arts that Lucy had absorbed in recent times seemed to have given her confidence beyond her years.

"We'll wash the wound as clean as we can. We want to be able to see fresh blood, but we can't let too much out as he's lost a lot already. See? His skin looks pale. We need to bind it tight and then, when we get him home and settled, we can dress and stitch the wound closed."

Maggie smiled. Her daughter was growing up. She seemed to have found a calling that settled and focussed her restless and clumsy energy. Maggie shuddered. Despite the mud that had initially saved Barney's life, she knew that Lucy was correct. Without the wound being cleaned, infection would set in and the life of the boy, whose head lay in her lap, would come to an agonising end.

Realising that her daughter, who was pressing down on the wound with both hands, was looking at her with her head cocked to the side as if waiting for a response, she replied, "Ye be keeping pressure on that wound while I tear the hem from my skirt. We'll pack it and bind it firm."

As the cart jolted along, Maggie and Lucy did their best to clean and stabilise the wound. Working together, they tore strips from the hem of Maggie's skirt before they temporarily and tightly bound the wound. The flow of blood slowed but did not stop. Silently they prayed that their efforts would not be in vain.

Some three hours later Barney lay on a straw pallet in the barn while Maggie and Lucy took it in turns to cool his fever with cold compresses. They tried their best to get him to drink cool water and clear soup through a funnel pressed between his dried lips, but despite their care, Barney's breathing continued to slow as his heart began to fail.

Over the course of a week, Barney's mind progressively became more and more detached from the prison of his fever-ridden body. It pecked at the boundaries of reality in an attempt to escape its cumbersome entrapment. Finally, in a singular instant of time, when his delirium consumed his consciousness, his mind managed to free itself. One moment he was scorched with pain and burning with fever and in the next he was hovering above his body, observing it from a detached perspective.

Then it was as if he were lifted up through the roof of the barn by a thermal column of air that drifted invisibly across the land. His mind gave him wings to try to explain his ability to fly while the fading lucid part of his brain vainly attempted to press him back towards the ground. When he looked again, the land was but a speck below him. Part of him revelled in his newfound freedom.

Barney soared above the land. Detached from the needs of his body, he wondered at his newfound freedom. Freedom to think, to dream, to remember and to be in the moment without any reason to consider the desires of others or even the needs of his own body. Why worry about food when he was defined by knowledge, and his memories were his own to reimagine? He had everything that he required. All he had ever needed to do was free himself from the confines of his own flesh.

He considered with scorn the efforts of those below him who sought to tame nature by attempting to bring it to heel beneath farms, roads and buildings. All they were doing was a vain attempt to serve the needs of their flesh. They couldn't halt the regrowth of weeds in their own fields, their aging or the ravages of time. Why suffer to secure the future, when it was possible to live like him, free of concern and free of pain? The euphoria of his discovery shimmered through him. The pettiness of those below him was beyond his contempt. As he glided over the land, his curiosity began to focus on its geography. His flight slowed as his subconscious began to regurgitate its knowledge, anything to cause him to pause and return to his body. Now, as he looked down, echoes of the tales that his father had told to him filtered through the fog of his flighted illusion and began to coalesce.

According to his father, the King was forever travelling out from the Citadel to quell uprisings and civil disobedience and to settle disputes arising from disagreements among the six nobles whom he and his ancestors had installed in each of the Kingdom's six counties.

Barney found himself looking down at a map of the Kingdom of the Six Counties as his conscious mind and subconscious mind fought for control. The knowledge passed to him by his father, and the tutors whom the Baron had engaged to teach anyone who would serve him, came unbidden to him.

The Kingdom was bordered by an ocean that extended from the shoreline to the horizon on three sides. It was only to the north that the Kingdom bordered the lands of another people. The two counties that bordered the Northern lands were administered by Baron Aethelson, whom Barney's father had served, and Duke Jacoby, who was the King's youngest and only surviving sibling.

These two counties were separated from the rest of the Kingdom by a spiny mountain range that, apart from one significant pass, isolated the Baron and the Duke from the King's influence. The squabbles between the Baron and the Duke were legendary. Those troubles, coupled with maintaining an active army to secure the Northern Border, meant that the two Northern Counties were amongst the poorest of the Kingdom.

To defend the Kingdom from its Northern neighbour, the King and his predecessors had constructed a series of fortifications along the entire border. The castles belonging to the Baron and the Duke were two of these fortifications.

As soon as Barney's thoughts turned to the Baron's castle it was as if the stone ramparts and its surrounding town of Landsend grew out of the map below him. The Baron's castle had been constructed in a natural basin valley. It acted as a secondary line of defence to protect one of the Kingdom's major northern gateways from the armies of the North.

Along the mountainous border a series of towers, walls and fortifications stood sentinel. The chain of fortifications was so extensive that the populace simply referred to it as "the Wall" even though the inhospitable terrain prevented the construction of a continuous line of defence.

On rare occasions before the Wall had been completed, the Northern Clans had united into one large invasion force under a war chief. Aided by surprise and ferocity, the progress of the Northern Horde's attacks had been marked by initial bloodied success. On one occasion they had conquered three of the six counties and captured the King, before their foothold in the Kingdom had been taken back from them.

Barney's mind flickered to childish visions of hordes of giants descending on his homeland from the North. For a while, he had acted out the part of a knight slaying the invaders, but in truth, it had been a long time since the Northern Horde had launched a full-scale attack.

Barney suddenly found himself at his father's feet listening to his analysis of the supposed weaknesses of the Northern Clans. His father had been convinced that the Northern Clans were weak as they had no true central government and this made it difficult for them to undertake a unified attack. Apparently, this was also a source of frustration for the King, as the lack of a central government made it difficult to negotiate with the Northerners. No sooner had peace been made with one of the clans than another clan would raid in its place.

Historically, the Northerners were without a united army that was prepared to lay siege for lengthy periods. Their way was that of the sword in open battle, in which the prowess of the warrior could be measured by how well the individual could wield a blade, not by whether they could sustain a lengthy period of encampment while besieging enemy fortifications to deny their enemy supplies and reinforcements. No one clan felt loyalty to another. Unless a war chief was appointed by all the clans, it was not punishable or wrong for one clan to abandon their battlefield responsibilities. War was a choice of the individual clans who, in the absence of a war chief, could determine, at any time, that their clan would be better served if their warriors were elsewhere.

Barney felt his father's pride in the fact that the Kingdom of the Six Counties was ruled over by one king. The King was the ultimate power with the responsibility for the management of issues that affected the whole Kingdom, including any dispute between the counties. In theory, the King based important decisions on the advice of the Council of the six individual nobles who governed the day-to-day lives of the people in the six counties.

A picture of his father's lifeless body seeped into Barney's mind, and suddenly he was escaping reality again, the thermals twitching at the feathers on his wingtips as he rose higher and higher above the land. He could see the vast mountain range in which the Northern Clans were reported to live. It was the sheer cliffs and deep valleys that made it almost impossible for any army to attack without being seen. It had been proven many times that the Northern Clans could defend their position by simply blocking the narrow mountain paths and rolling boulders down from the cliffs to impede the attacking forces.

A stalemate, punctuated by minor skirmishes, was now the accepted norm along the Northern Border.

The features of the land below Barney were diminishing and the pain was becoming a distant memory, but he could still hear and feel a slight breeze. That breeze carried with it an unfamiliar voice that mocked his efforts to escape reality.

Barney's breath had grown to be softer than that of a sleeping newborn baby. The fiery red of the wound and its surrounds contrasted with the sickening whiteness of the rest of his person. Sighing to herself, Maggie leaned in close to

Barney's ear with tears in her eyes. After tenderly brushing his hair to one side, she gently blew on his forehead as if to cool him and then she whispered softly with sadness in her voice, "So that be it then. Ye be giving up."

Barney's flight hesitated. He paused just as the colours of the landscape below him were blending into one. His fragmented consciousness began to reform around the words. He hated being accused of giving up on anything. In life, he was far too stubborn to leave any worthy chore unfinished. Barney prided himself on only ever choosing the course of action that he regarded as being the best and most efficient way to logically address an issue. To him no decision was ever wrong or easy if it achieved the desired outcome. From deep inside, Barney drew on a well of stubbornness that he had inherited from his mother. It was time for him to wake up.

He closed his eyes and shut out the light. He channelled his anger and the despair that arose from his inability to change the direction of his flight. He hovered as he fought for control of himself. Then he felt himself falling, slowly at first and then faster and faster, until he felt the pain of his wound and finally the unrelenting heat of his fever. But now it was different. Now he had a purpose. He would prove the voice wrong, and he would look the speaker in the eye and tell her that he had not given up.

The voice came to him again, but this time it dripped with hope. "That's it, lad. Fight!"

In his mind, Barney opened his eyes, but all the colour of the world was gone. He could see nothing. Everything and everywhere was black. He felt a primeval sound rise in his throat. Finally, it escaped his lips. His anguished cry rent the air as his muscles contracted, forcing him to sit up. Then he felt at peace and the deepest of sleeps began to claim him.

Maggie saw Barney's body tense before his terrible and uncontrollable shivering began again. The boy screamed something incomprehensible and unholy before his body stilled itself as if the chills from the fever had been banished.

Chuckling, Maggie gently kissed Barney's brow before whispering, "That's it, child; come back to the world. It ain't all that bad."

FOUR

—— ✦ ——

Barney slept for two days while his exhausted body recovered from the ravaging effects of the fever. When he opened his eyes, he discovered himself to be lying on a straw pallet under a coarse grey woollen blanket in an old barn. Somewhere a cock was crowing, and the birds were singing to encourage the sun to rise.

Barney felt lost and confused. He had no idea where he was or how he had got there. From somewhere beyond his toes, he made out the quick padding of bare feet passing by. Someone else was in the barn. As his vision cleared, he lay still and watched as a short young girl with shoulder-length light brown hair ran past carrying a basket of eggs.

"Hello," he said.

Well, that's what he thought he'd said. All the girl heard was a croak coming from the direction of the boy she thought to be dying. Startled, she turned, looked, misjudged where she was going and ran headfirst into a support pillar. The eggs flew in all directions. Barney felt the unmistakable feeling of yolk dripping onto his face from one of the eggs that had shattered on the wall behind him.

The girl rose unsteadily to her feet as a lump on her forehead started to swell.

"Ma, come quick, he's alive!" she yelled. Then she giggled at the sight of the yolk sliding down Barney's face.

A very short, stout, dark-haired woman, who reminded Barney of his Aunt Bess appeared. The woman was all business as she strode through the door towards Barney, but when she saw that his eyes were open, she smiled. The smile made her eyes shine and softened her look and, in that moment, Barney knew that he was safe.

"Lucy, fetch some cool water. The bairn in me barn is awake." Her voice was anything but melodious. It was a typical country accent from the area where shouting long distances in the fields was common.

Barney tried to smile and then opened his mouth as if to speak.

"Hush child. There'll be no sound from ye till you've wet your lips."

The girl eventually came back, bearing a jug of water.

"Well, what ye be gawking at! Clean the mess you've made. Collect the eggs that ain't broke and finish your chores."

Barney thought it was strange that the woman had seemed unconcerned about the swelling on Lucy's forehead. He was to learn that Lucy's scrapes, cuts and bruises occurred so often that her family had stopped noticing them.

A small ceramic cup was pressed against his lips.

"Easy. No gulping or ye'll throw it up."

Frustratingly slowly the beautiful liquid trickled over his lips, along his tongue and down his throat. Until that moment Barney had not realised how thirsty he was. One cup later he was exhausted by the effort, and he once again fell asleep.

Gradually, as the days went on, Barney progressed from water to broth and then to mushed food which was fed to him by either Maggie or Lucy.

Barney grew to recognise Maggie's deliberate footsteps and Lucy's light but haphazard footfalls. Despite welcoming Maggie's presence, he found himself to be fascinated by Lucy, who would often speak from the moment she entered the barn until after she left. Indeed, sometimes, when she appeared to disregard his presence, she would greet each chicken by name or muse out loud about a sunrise or a distant tree. Try as he might, Barney was unable to concentrate on all that was said to him. He was often caught off guard by a sudden query that was directed his way simply because he had difficulty following Lucy's commentary. In response she would smile, sometimes sadly, and then launch into the answer.

Lucy's intense chattering was only ever punctuated with queries about his health. These questions, and his answers, were clearly important to her and she would wait for his response, with her head tilted slightly to the side and her big brown eyes entirely focussed on him. Hours and sometimes days would then pass before she would suddenly refer to his answers as if she had written them down.

The silent void that accompanied Barney was shattered each and every time Lucy came within hearing distance.

It was late in the afternoon and one of the more inquisitive chickens had landed on his blankets. Without thinking Barney motioned at it. "Henrietta, get down! Go away."

From the doorway Barney heard a delighted giggle. He turned to see Lucy in the doorway with what looked to be a bundle of clothing. Barney blushed a crimson red.

"Glad to see that you are finally getting acquainted. Time to change. Henrietta seems to have taken a liking to you. Don't be surprised if you wake up to an egg on your blanket. Did you know—"

"Why do you want me to get changed?"

"Ma says it will freshen you up and make you feel better. Besides, you smell bad."

He got in quickly with a second question. "Where do the clothes come from?"

Lucy's eyes glazed over with the first sign of the tears that would obviously flow if he pressed the issue any further. "They belong to my brother. Marcus was taken to serve in the King's army on the Wall. We haven't heard from him for a long, long time." Her voice dropped to a whisper. "It's been so long. I don't think he'll be back."

Barney felt guilty as he lifted the clothes from where Lucy had placed them. To steer the subject away from Marcus he replied, "I don't think I've seen your sister around."

Lucy's face twisted into a smile, "As far as Shine is concerned, what's in the barn stays in the barn. I like caring for the animals, so I get to feed, clean and water them. Shine has other skills. If she could move to a town and be a seamstress, she would. Da won't let her leave 'cos she's too young. They butt heads a bit seeing as they are so alike. Shine won't be visiting you anytime soon. I'm not sure why she wants to leave the clean open living of the farm for all the crowds of people. Perhaps it's the shops. How boring. Honestly, how could anybody actually want to spend their lives having to buy everything? There're so many better ways to spend your time. Out here we have nearly everything we need and what we don't have we can make or get when we take our wheat to market. No one here notices if you're wearing last year's fashion. Granted, she's a wonderful seamstress. I'm actually wearing—"

As Lucy took a breath she noticed that Barney was staring at her with mouth agape trying to process the information. She blushed a deep red, spun on the spot and hurried from the barn.

"Wait..."

"Sorry, got to go. Chores to do."

Barney watched her leave and wondered whether he would ever be able to keep up with her rapid progression of ideas and speech.

Farmer Tom only paid two visits to see Barney; once to see if he was alive and a second to tell him that when he was fit and well, he was expected to work off his debt before leaving the farm. Barney was not sure how much his debt was, or how much his labour was worth. He simply nodded and smiled as he was in no condition to argue the point.

There came a day, some three weeks after he arrived when Lucy skipped to his bedside. "Ma said you are to come to the table for tea. Da doesn't like it 'cos he says you're the help and you've done nothing to help 'cos all you do is just eat and sleep. Ma said you are to come anyway 'cos it's her house too and as she cooked the food, she can give it to whoever she pleases. Ma sent me to get you." Lucy stopped and cocked her head expectantly, waiting for a response.

Barney was totally confused. He didn't want to do anything to antagonise Farmer Tom, but sooner or later he had to get up and about and leave the barn. Grimacing, he stood, testing his ankle which failed to unduly protest. Then he sat back down to let a sudden wave of nausea subside. Lucy stood over him. For once she wasn't fidgeting or even talking. Barney felt like he was being assessed.

"Lean on me if you want to."

Barney stubbornly shook his head, "I'll be right in a moment."

Lucy's pupils dilated, whether from annoyance or concern Barney didn't know. Grounding his feet, he stood.

Lucy smiled. She waited long enough to ensure that he was able to follow her before she skipped on ahead of him.

Just inside the barn there was a cleared space about a small table that nested between two bales of hay.

Barney stopped for a moment and braced himself on the table. Glancing over the table, he caught sight of a small stack of parchment that was weighted down by a handy rock. Resting beside it were two quills, their bottled ink by their side. Looking closer, he could see line after line of the same text. It reminded him of the lines of writing that the Baron's scribes had made him practise so that he might be qualified to enter the Baron's service. The writing was far neater than his own.

"What's up?" asked Lucy, who had popped her head around the doorframe. Concern was written on her face.

"Sorry. I didn't mean to spy."

"That's Shine's. Says she needs peace and quiet when she practises. Mine's in the house. I come out here sometimes, but I prefer to do it inside or down near the stream or there's a really nice tree—"

She glanced up to see that Barney was clearly waiting politely for her to go on. No one ever waited for her to speak. She shook her head. "Shine was accepted as part of the Baron's program. As I told you earlier, she wants to move into town. Da can't object if the Baron sends for her to enter into his service, but the Baron won't accept anyone in his service unless they can read and write. Makes them more useful, I expect. She found out that I had started to learn so the very next time she saw the Baron's travelling scribe in Marydale, she marched right up to him and wouldn't leave until he had agreed to teach her. Ma's not too keen on the idea. Says she can't see why Shine needs to read and write if all she has got to do is to tend the farm or make clothes. After a time, Shine started to speak different. Says she wants to fit in at court.

"I am not being taught by the scribes. I was with the Healer, recovering from a dislocated shoulder, and was quizzing him on how he knew what to do to treat me. He tossed me some written records. Said that to remind himself he wrote down what worked so that he could do the same thing over and over. I couldn't read, you see. It looked pretty but didn't make any sense. It felt like I was missing out. The next time the Healer and his wife sat down to give their children lessons, I joined in. Now, when I'm at the Healer's place I can read his parchments. I have learned a lot of things from the words and not just about treating ailments. Someday I'm going to be just as good as him. Come on. If the food goes cold before we get there we'll be in trouble."

Barney shuffled forward, not quite trusting his own feet. He knew that Baron Aethelson had commissioned a small, select group of his scribes to travel throughout his County to teach whoever they deemed fit so that they might be able to be taken into the Baron's service, but he had never met anyone from it. He knew that apart from children, like himself, who were expected to follow in their parent's footsteps and serve the Baron, outsider candidates needed to demonstrate a way of thinking or a skill that would enhance the knowledge of the Baron's court and not simply repeat what was already known. He wondered what the Baron's scribe could possibly have seen in Shine when she had first approached him.

As he followed Lucy he also idly recalled the rule that the Baron would only permit one child of a farming family to learn so that there would always be enough farmers to feed his county and enough conscripts for the army. He wondered whether the scribe knew that Lucy had also found a way to learn to read and write.

The homestead was the central building of a sprawling farm complex which consisted of numerous sheds, a stable for the horses that were used to pull various carts and to haul the plough, a store for harvested crops and many other miscellaneous buildings, the use of which Barney was unable to guess. He had never been on a farm before. All the buildings were made of wood and had thatched roofs. Surrounding the complex were fields of wheat flowing over the hilly landscape in a way that, to Barney's eyes, appeared random. A more knowledgeable person would have understood that Farmer Tom was taking advantage of natural drainage and the contours of the land to protect the crop and reduce the work that was needed to manage the farm.

Following Lucy's lead, Barney removed his boots before he entered the cottage. As he stepped inside, he stopped to gawk at the most homely and colourful building that he had ever been in. The interior was divided into three main areas: the kitchen, living room and the sleeping quarters.

Everywhere he looked, colourful quilts and wildflowers adorned the walls and the ceiling rafters, creating a riot of colour that both intrigued and welcomed him at the same time. Given Shine's desire to be a seamstress Barney guessed that the quilts were Shine's handiwork while the flowers were likely to have been sourced by Lucy due to her confessed love of nature. In comparison, Barney's home was plain and utilitarian. Everything had a practical purpose.

"Sit and be welcome," said Maggie, disturbing his thoughts with both what she said and her wide and welcoming smile. "And tell us about yerself."

So, while Tom glowered at the head of the table and Shine completely ignored him, Barney hesitantly directed his tale towards Maggie and Lucy.

"I live in the old part of Landsend next to the Baron's fortress. My father is a member of the guards. He was busted from officer of the watch twice on account of him drinking on duty. My mother washes and mends the clothing of the Baron's men-at-arms. I have no sisters or brothers. My parents are good folk. Despite me being their only child, they have allowed me to learn to read and write from the Baron's scribes so that I might be of value to the Baron. My father believes that I would make a better scribe than a fighter, on account of me not being naturally strong or any good with a sword."

"Why were you in Tom's field?" prompted Maggie.

"My father was sent out on patrol after reports that some outlaws were roaming the area. My mother told me to go with them so that I might learn something of my future given that even the Baron's scribes have to be able to undertake the duties of the Baron's watch. I'd only left the town for very short journeys in the country before, to fairs and the like, so it was exciting to be in the country.”

Barney paused.

“Is my father dead?”

There was silence at the table. Shine flicked her raven black hair away from her face so that she was able to look directly at him. “Yes,” she said simply. It was the first time that she had addressed him.

Barney had seen the black arrow, the blood and his father’s sightless eyes, but until that moment he had tried to convince himself that it had been a dream, a nightmare caused by his fever. Tears welled in his eyes. He glared at Shine.

“What did he look like?” pressed Maggie, to distract him from the confrontation with her outspoken and moody daughter that she could sense was inevitably coming. Why Shine was always so rude after she returned from Marydale was something that Maggie had difficulty understanding.

Barney couldn’t think past the arrow that had killed his father. He couldn’t recall his father’s height or the colour of his eyes. “He was killed by a black arrow through his neck,” was all that he could blurt out.

Tom recalled the man. He was, at that very moment, wearing the man’s boots. Rising, he crossed to the stove and lifted a small wooden box from the shelf above it. He came towards Barney as he rummaged around in it. “This be yours then,” he said as he placed on the table a silver embossed signet ring that had been Barney’s father’s pride and joy.

Barney picked up the ring and burst into tears. His father was truly dead, and he had no idea how he would break the news to his mother.

The next day, at Maggie's insistence, Lucy hitched a buggy to a horse and drove Barney out to the site of the skirmish. Bitza rode in the back.

Lucy's talking was like an angry bee as she detailed her exploits in the area. She spoke of the many places to see wondrous flowers and insects. Barney nodded every now and again and smiled when Lucy paused slightly. He found that if he stopped listening and concentrated on the movement of the wheat as it flowed in the wind on either side of the path, he could remove himself from the present, and thoughts of the future, to a place where there was no pain or uncertainty.

It took some time to reach the lone oak tree that marked his father's resting place. By then, Barney was so distracted that it wasn't until Lucy finally stopped talking that he realised they had arrived.

The grass and wheat had begun to recover from the trampling that it had received. A stubble of weeds had already appeared along a long scar of freshly dug earth that identified the last resting place of the patrol.

Barney didn't know what to do. He had already cried tears of loss and sorrow. Now he stood before the grave trying to remember the good times, the laughter, and every other detail of his father. He strove to carve an indelible image in his memory that would not be eroded by time lest the betrayal of forgetting any singular aspect of his parent taunt him. Strangely, he felt more grief about never seeing his father again than anger about what had occurred.

He must have been standing and thinking for some time because it wasn't until Lucy tugged on his arm that he realised she had been talking to him, "Come, we must go now; if we don't get home before dark Da will get mad."

Nodding, Barney stooped and picked up a handful of dirt. He stood and let it run through his fingers. Goodbye Dad, he thought, before his hand went to his pocket to roll the pawn between his fingers.

Turning, he looked at Lucy, "I must return to my mother to tell her about all of this."

"Da will help."

Well before they arrived back in sight of the homestead the sun had lost most of its warmth as it crept towards the horizon. As the air about them cooled, Barney didn't give his own discomfort a second thought when he removed his jacket and slid it around Lucy's shoulders. She glanced up at him with gratitude, teeth chattering violently, holding the reins.

"Sorry for keeping us out this long."

Lucy smiled at him with the same welcoming, honest, and radiant smile of her mother. She instantly forgave him as they huddled closer together to share some warmth.

They arrived home just as Farmer Tom was about to go and look for them. "Tomorrow, you work," he said to Barney.

"Tomorrow, I must start looking for my mother so that I can tell her what happened."

"Humph. You think it would be safe for you to travel alone? Which way would you go? Tomorrow, you work."

Barney had no idea how to respond. He needed to find his mother, but Farmer Tom was correct. He had no idea where he was. He had taken no notice of the route the patrol had taken. Barney realised that his inattention had left him in a vulnerable position. He was furious at himself and silently he promised that he would never make that mistake again.

Before he could reply, Maggie came to his rescue, "Thomas, he'll work for two months and then he'll come with us to market at Marydale. It ain't that far from the markets to the town. We can take him to his mother before or after market. It matters not. But he'll be coming. No mother should be deprived of her son and with his father in the ground, he'll need to step up."

Barney knew that Maggie was referring to her own son. It was easy to see that Farmer Tom would not be winning the argument. Farmer Tom seemed to resign himself to his inevitable loss. He grunted before nodding his head and stepping back inside.

Farmer Tom met Barney outside the barn the next morning at dawn, just as the cock crowed. Over his shoulder, he carried the longest and sharpest axe that Barney had ever seen. He grunted at Barney and gestured for him to follow to the woodpile.

"Before breakfast, make a start on these logs. Split 'em so that they can be used as kindling in the kitchen. You used an axe before?"

Barney nodded. He was confident in his ability to undertake this chore. It was one that he'd done daily for his mother.

Farmer Tom handed Barney the axe and Barney stepped up to the chopping block and balanced a large log on it.

As he swung the axe high above his head, his left arm crumpled. The axe head fell to the ground perilously close to Farmer Tom, who cuffed him angrily across the back of his head. Barney realised that when the knife had struck him below his left shoulder, it must have severely damaged his ability to lift anything above head height.

"I'm so sorry. I'm not sure what happened. My arm gave way. It's never happened before. I wasn't trying to harm you."

Farmer Tom considered the boy for a moment. There was no hint of malice or mockery; the boy's distress appeared open and honest. Farmer Tom took up a piece of wood and handed it to Barney, "Lift it with yer right arm above yer head and then switch to yer left."

Once again, Barney's left arm collapsed, but this time there was a flash of pain.

Farmer Tom probed the area of the knife wound with his fingers, comparing it with the right side of Barney's chest. He noticed immediately that something didn't feel right. Farmer Tom also noted that although Barney grimaced at his invasive probing, he did not back away. He made a mental note that there might be more to Barney than the sickly and scrawny youth standing before him.

He stepped back and directed Barney to try to raise a small log above his head with his left arm while he maintained pressure on the area of the wound. As the log passed his ear, Barney felt his arm weaken and then he found that he had to strain to straighten it. Farmer Tom could feel the muscle and tissue give way under his fingertips. The log dropped to the ground.

Tom sighed. The injury was likely to hold the boy back from doing anything useful for his entire life. "Every day, three times a day, you'll come to this woodpile. You'll lift and hold a piece of wood above your head. If you ain't near this woodpile, find somethin' else of similar size and weight. Start light but then keep increasin' the weight. Lift the log slowly up and down; go for control, not speed. Do it at least three times. If you can lift the log fifteen times in a row, then next time go heavier. Mind you do both arms so ya keep the balance. Ya left shoulder will probably never be as it was, but ya need to retrain it. It's now yar life's challenge, boy. Gain strength and teach yar body to adapt or ya won't be able to use yer arm and ya'll be nothing more than a burden to ya mother. Ya'll have to work that much harder to replace yar father as the man of yar household. Accept the injury but not the weakness. Ya'll need two arms to get you by.

"For the moment I'll do the choppin' and you be doing the carryin'. Take it to the kitchen. I'll be sharpenin' the hatchet for ya to use on the morrow. Well, what ya be gawkin' at? Let's be gettin' to it!"

Barney was more than a little shocked. At first, the meaning and importance of Farmer Tom's words did not sink in. It had been by far the longest speech that Tom had ever made to him!

For the next two months, Barney worked harder than he ever had before. He learned to clean the stables, hitch a horse to the wagon, water and feed the animals, collect the eggs, chop the firewood and care for the crops. His days were full and a complete distraction from his thoughts about his future meeting with his mother. He now realised that it would fall to him to make the money that was needed for them to live, and, with his injury, his options were truly limited. They would have to move, but he did not know where they could go.

Each night, beside his bed, he found a bowl of a thick white milky substance and instructions directing him to rub it into his blisters to prevent infection. After a while, a green substance also appeared. This he was to use on his shoulder. Although the green liquid was cool, it seemed to heat his skin from the inside out. On one occasion, Barney made the mistake of rubbing his tired eyes after applying the green ointment to his shoulder. The resultant pain caused him to run out into the yard where he dunked his head into a water trough. He surfaced to the laughter of Farmer Tom, Maggie and Shine. Lucy stood to one side, tapping her foot with a stern look on her face as if annoyed at his foolishness. Barney's eyes were partially swollen shut for two days.

Barney was grateful, yet disappointed, to be leaving his new life on the idyllic farm when Farmer Tom announced after dinner one evening that they would set off on their journey to Marydale on the morrow. He remained grateful even when Farmer Tom made it clear that Barney had to stay up late that night to check the harness of the family wagon to ensure that it was not too worn.

They loaded the wagon with sacks of produce in dawn's early light and set off as the sun was still struggling to get above the horizon. Barney and Lucy sat in the back of the wagon with their backs resting on the sacks and their legs dangling over the edge while Maggie and Shine sat on the driver's bench discussing what they needed from town. Farmer Tom rode beside them all on a short stocky horse that had seen better days. As she was known to roam, they left Bitza with friends on an adjoining farm.

Barney was prepared to sit and rest in the wagon; however, Lucy was filled with impatience and the desire to run. Before the first hour was up, she had convinced Barney to walk beside the wagon. When that didn't satisfy her, she stole his hat.

"Bet you can't catch me before the next rise in the road!"

Barney was unfit and Lucy was quick, very, very quick. She ensured that she stayed just ahead of Barney. No matter how much he tried, he couldn't catch her until she finally slipped on some wet ground, falling heavily onto the grass beside the road and knocking the wind out of herself.

"Give it back," Barney snapped as he sat on top of Lucy and snatched at his hat.

"Get off, you oaf! Only playing."

All Barney wanted to do was to push her further into the mud, but her cheeky grin made him think twice. Retrieving his hat, he slid off Lucy and they sat beside the road waiting for the wagon to catch up.

"You're soooo slooooow," she laughed.

Barney smiled as he puffed. "No, you're just faster."

His admission delighted Lucy and threw her into a spasm of fresh laughter. It was infectious and soon spread to him. As he laughed, Barney realised that he hadn't laughed since before his father had been struck down. The thought saddened him and subdued his mood.

As Tom pulled alongside, he gestured to the two, "Walk beside us," he said.

Barney rose to his feet and held out his hand to help Lucy, who held his eyes with hers as she rose, "We're all going to miss you. Da could do with a hand. You and your mother should consider staying with us."

Barney frowned but didn't respond. Just as he couldn't see himself in the Baron's employ as a guardsman, he couldn't see himself as a farmer. He looked away from Lucy as he walked beside the wagon.

Lucy pursed her lips. Then she shrugged her shoulders and caught up with Barney. As they walked, Lucy talked about everything she saw, from the wildflowers to the different types of crops in the fields beside the road. She even explained how the slope of the land was used to favour certain crops and how water could be channelled to the crops. Barney listened with only half an ear and hardly spoke at all as there was relatively little silence to fill.

Every now and then Lucy would dart off to pick some flowers, a leaf, or an entire plant and slip them carefully into a satchel that she carried over her back. The family ignored her antics. Barney assumed that the collection was to be made into a garland for Lucy's hair or perhaps decorations for the wagon, but after she brought back some roots he finally bothered to ask her what they were for.

The instant his question passed his lips, a thoughtful demeanour settled over Lucy and her movements calmed. Her rambling discourse ceased and her brow furrowed as she changed the topic to the medicinal properties of the roots that she was holding and the other plants that she had gathered.

Eventually, there was a pause in Lucy's discourse and Barney managed to interject before she could start again, "So you made the lotions for my blisters and my shoulder?"

"Is that really all that you've got out of what I've been saying? Of course I did! Remember how you took to collecting the eggs and doing a lot of chores in the barn? Well, they were my chores. You doing them gave me the time that I needed to gather the things necessary to restock our herb supplies so that they'd be ready if anyone becomes sick or injured. Honestly, do you think that all the ingredients just appear?"

Barney looked to Maggie for confirmation. Maggie simply nodded her head.

"Well, thank you for helping me."

Lucy had stopped and was looking at him with her head tilted to one side as if considering his words or waiting for something further. When Barney proffered nothing more she shrugged. "No problem. I enjoy making cures. I tried some new ones that I had learned from the Healer on you and wasn't quite sure if I had got the ingredients right. I am now writing down descriptions of every treatment that I know together with my observations on their success. See!" She thrust at him a wad of loosely bound quires of paper.

Barney took the quires from Lucy and gently thumbed through them. He recognised some of the treatments, particularly the description of the green ointment. He noted that in its margin there was a fresh note to "warn the patient to keep it away from their eyes".

Barney didn't know whether he should be annoyed by her having experimented on him or just grateful that the preparations seemed to have worked. The descriptions were incredibly detailed although the drawings of the plants would need some practice. He handed the bundles of paper back to Lucy, "That's great work. Once again, thank you."

"You really think it's good?"

Barney nodded. "Really good."

Lucy blushed at the praise and for a short time she was actually silent. The moment quickly passed and she thrust the papers back into her satchel before she hung off his arm to continue her discourse as if she had never been interrupted. From the wagon, Shine rolled her eyes.

Lucy had not spent all of her time working on the farm, fulfilling the role of a farmer's daughter. Maggie had shown her how to cook from almost the moment she could walk, but because of Lucy's clumsiness, Maggie also had to show Lucy how to make cooling lotions for burns, and antiseptic poultices for cuts and bruises.

According to Lucy, she had recently been "lucky enough" to spend nearly three months with the Healer in Marydale while she was recovering from a particularly nasty fall. During her time in Marydale, the Healer had kept her busy and, perhaps Barney thought, to keep her quiet, learning the healing properties of many different plants. Over a relatively short time, Lucy's enthusiasm had led to her memorising and categorising the ingredients required for many treatments. When she returned to the farm, Lucy had begun collecting and experimenting with any new type of plant she found to see if it had any healing properties.

Once the Healer had heard and seen evidence of Lucy's growing prowess, he had started to use the farm as a base while he was on his travels, and when he was there, he encouraged Lucy to expand her knowledge. After witnessing

Lucy apply her newly acquired knowledge and skills to Barney's care, Maggie now openly admitted that her own knowledge had been well and truly surpassed by Lucy. Although Maggie had initially applied the poultices to Barney's wound, it was Lucy who had mixed the poultices to draw out the poisons resulting from the infection. Lucy had tried everything that she knew to speed his recovery.

Barney reflected on his mother's now-thwarted belief that he had been destined to follow in his father's footsteps. Lucy had, perhaps unintentionally, opened a choice of futures by simply taking advantage of events and doing what came naturally to her.

Barney found the more he thought about Lucy's skills, the more he respected his companion for taking the opportunity to learn. Her enthusiasm and willingness to share sparked and held his fascination. He had never met anyone quite like her. Despite not understanding a lot of what she said, he had found a reason to listen to her as she lovingly described, in exquisite detail, the medicinal qualities of plants.

They were less than a day from Marydale when the party camped for the night in a clearing beside the road. Unusually, for such a large and well-known campsite, there was no one else there. Before they turned in for the night Farmer Tom went to the wagon. After rummaging around, he came back to Barney and threw a log at Barney's feet.

"Three times a day is what I said."

He nodded and then went to lie down. Barney sighed, realising that for the first time he had forgotten his exercise routine. Why was it, he thought, people only ever noticed when he forgot to do something?

No one else had joined them at the campsite by the time they were ready to set off the next day. Tom said nothing of his unease, but he recalled that the boy's father had been on patrol looking for bandits. While considering whether they should turn back to the safety of his farm, he kicked the soil to ensure that the remaining coals were smothered by earth.

He looked over at his family and the boy. He had grown fond of Barney, despite himself. He watched as the boy winced through his morning exercise routine. He was able to bear more weight than when he had first started the exercises, but Tom knew that in a scrap Barney wouldn't be much assistance. Despite his stubborn nature, the boy just didn't have Marcus's strength.

Tom checked his thoughts before they led him down the dark path of wondering what might have happened to his son. Without Maggie's knowledge he had posted a reward for information, but useful information was yet to come. Tom knew where Marcus had been sent, but he was unable to secure any further intelligence.

The boy wasn't a shirker and he had done well on the farm. Perhaps Lucy was right: the boy would need employment to support his mother and in Marcus's absence the family could sure do with some help.

Tom watched as his eldest daughter flicked her hair impatiently from where she already sat on the driver's seat waiting for Maggie. Shine was the polar opposite of her younger sister. Tom knew why Shine preferred to be in Marydale, but he would wait for Shine to tell her mother. It was not his place to tell her and, besides, Shine was needed on the farm. The time would come soon enough when Shine would leave them, and he didn't want to do anything that might hasten that event.

He smiled somewhat wistfully as Lucy darted about the clearing. He was almost certain that Lucy would like to stay on the farm, but in her he could see a need for her to adopt a cause: to care for a wound or care for a heart. Tom wondered when the Healer might draw him aside to talk of apprenticing Lucy to him. He would make sure that the conversation was delayed for as long as possible because he was uncertain how he would answer.

He looked with affection as Maggie drew herself up onto the driver's seat and took the reins from Shine's hands. His wife had been with him through thick and thin. Maggie was part of him, but sooner or later they would be left alone on the farm and eventually age would wrong-foot them, and it would become too much for them to work and pay the Baron what he was due. When they could no longer pay, they would be moved on, or even worse, sent to debtors' prison. With sadness, Tom knew that change was coming. Perhaps one of his daughters would marry a farmer and stay on the farm to inherit it, but his heart was heavy with doubt.

Tom shook his head to relieve himself of his melancholy and strode to his horse. No use thinking too much about what might be. Tomorrow would take care of itself and worrying wasn't going to help. The notion of them returning to the farm was forgotten.

Tom mounted his horse and motioned for Maggie to set off for Marydale. Turning at the sounds of delighted giggles, he watched his youngest daughter dart in and grab the boy's hat again before she ran on ahead with Barney in hot pursuit. Tom smirked. Perhaps there was hope for the farm, as unexpected as that source of help might be.

It was early afternoon when they came across tracks made by a large number of people. The wide, straight path dissected the meandering road and churned the earth as far as the eye could see. Trampled crops, broken fences and broken equipment stood as testament to many travellers having moved quickly and purposefully across the landscape.

"Da? What's happened here?" asked Lucy.

Tom stopped his horse. They all waited for his answer.

"I ain't sure. Not folk from hereabouts or there'd be a bounty on their heads for the damage. Possibly troops. Looks like they be heading to the Baron's castle. Could be foe. Could be the King's army coming to remind the Baron of something. I know nothin' of politics. I don't care for it. The tracks look like they bypass Marydale so we be headin' there for the night. Not riskin' another night in the open as there be no tellin' who be about. We'll return 'ome on the morrow. No point anyone takin' the time to bother us there."

Reaching into one of his saddlebags Tom brought out a sword that had belonged to a member of the Baron's patrol and hung it around his waist. Sitting taller in the saddle, he appeared alert but somewhat nervous.

"Keep an eye out. Lucy, shush! Listen out for anyone else. Shoulda brought Bitza."

For once Lucy managed to remain almost silent. After they began to notice signs of unusual activity, they grew more alert. Fruit trees had been stripped bare. Very few livestock were in the fields and the apiaries to the side of the road had been tipped over and emptied of their honey.

Marydale was usually a small sleepy village that served as a meeting place and a secondary market for the surrounding farms. It was too near Landsend and Baron Aethelson's castle to flourish as a major centre, so it functioned mainly as a final stop for farmers bringing produce to town and somewhere for those who had suffered farmyard injuries to be looked after. It was also a place where country folk could gather and gossip with old friends in the tavern. There was a single main street surrounded by short side streets that led to stables, the Healer's home and the thatched houses of the local residents.

Every other time Tom and his family had been to Marydale they had been welcomed by friends as if their arrival was the most exciting thing that had ever happened; that day, the village was very different. Due to its strategic location, the village was an ideal staging post for invaders. It was far enough from the Baron's castle to be safe while close enough to serve as a rear supply depot, marshalling area, and an infirmary for the wounded.

Approaching the village, Tom and the others could hear activity. As they came to the final rise in the road, they saw that Marydale was now a bustling centre. Throngs of people moved about tents that had been erected around the village. It was as if a nest of ants had been kicked over. Smoke belched from smithies and there was a cacophony of sound from the continual hammering, grinding, chopping and shouting. All manner of people were milling around; horses were being marshalled in large yards and wrestling and arms practice was occurring. There was movement everywhere.

Tom immediately stopped. "Turn 'round. Fast. We be leavin'."

At best, the wagon was cumbersome to turn around. To turn it completely and quickly around on a narrow country road was nigh on impossible. At Maggie's unusually insistent urging, the two horses hitched to the wagon became skittish and hard to control. Eventually, the wagon came to a standstill across the road with the wide-eyed horses refusing to budge.

From down the road, they heard the pounding of hoofbeats on the packed earthen road.

"Shine, Lucy, Barney! Into the bushes now!" commanded Tom tersely as he drew his sword.

As the three scampered off the road, eleven heavily armoured members of Duke Jacoby's cavalry cantered into sight.

"Halt," called the lead rider, raising his hand above his head.

The riders halted as one and spread across the road.

"We are sent to forage and find nothing of interest and then the gods deliver us produce," snickered the lead rider. "You'll not be harmed if you bring the wagon into the village with us. If you oppose us, you die right here and now. Your wagon and its contents are forfeit to the Duke."

Even though Tom knew little of war, he knew that these men would cut him and Maggie down without a second thought. He nodded.

"We'll follow," he said, as he sheathed his sword.

The riders didn't bother to disarm Tom or search Maggie for weapons, as they did not doubt their superiority. There was no way that the two farmers could resist them.

Tom and Maggie, without looking at the trio's hiding place, allowed the riders to assist them to straighten the wagon and then, with the cavalry encircling them, they set off with their escort towards the village.

Barney, Lucy and Shine stayed still and watched as the wagon and its guard moved off.

"Let's go," said Barney.

Lucy stood in front of him, "Follow me; I know this area well from collecting plants."

Barney nodded in agreement. Shine stayed down.

"Come on," said Barney.

"And the plan is?" Shine whispered curtly.

"We follow and find out where they go and watch what happens," Barney whispered back.

"Great plan. And we trust Lucy to lead us, do we?"

"Yes. We do. Unless you have an alternative course of action to suggest?"

Shine rose, refusing to look Barney in the eye. She had no desire to be left alone, but she doubted Lucy's capacity to lead them in the right direction.

They followed Lucy deeper into the undergrowth. As they crept away from the road and beneath the trees, the undergrowth thinned out and it became quicker and easier for them to move without making too much noise. Aligning herself with the dense foliage at the side of the road, where the canopy did not block the light from the ground, Lucy led them in a direction roughly parallel to the road to Marydale.

SEVEN

———— ✦ ————

Barney, Lucy and Shine watched from the edge of the forest as the wagon passed through a checkpoint and then slowly made its way towards the lines of tents. The activity in and around Marydale was ceaseless. Arrows were being fletched, armour repaired and manufactured, siege towers constructed, and healers were caring for the wounded. Tom and Maggie were being taken into an encampment that showed every sign of being the forward support base of the Duke's army.

Tom and Maggie weren't required to travel to the centre of Marydale. They were stopped just within the outer perimeter of tents beside a large, newly built structure from which they could hear the screams of animals being slaughtered for their meat.

The leader of the riders dismounted and went inside. After a short wait, he returned to direct his troop to take the wagon to a storage area further down the road. A tall man with long red hair stepped out as they drew near.

The red-haired man ignored Tom and Maggie. He went to the rear of the wagon, leapt on board and climbed on top of the sacks. He took a knife and, after randomly selecting a sack, he slit the cords that were binding it. He ran his hand through the bushels of wheat and then looked up at Tom.

"Thank you, farmer. Your produce will serve us well," he said as he jumped down from the cart.

Maggie cut off Tom's reply from her place on the driver's seat, "That'll be the Baron's wheat. We can't just be giving it to ya."

The man turned and looked at Maggie. Without a word he took three quick steps and leapt up beside her. Drawing back his fist, he drove it into the right side of Maggie's jaw. The punch lifted her from her seat and threw her from the wagon. She struck her head on the ground and came to rest, lying senseless beneath Tom's horse.

Tom reached for his sword.

The red-headed man shifted his weight, stood up on the driver's bench, balanced himself and flicked his knife at Tom. The tip of the knife buried itself into Tom's right bicep before his sword was out of its scabbard.

"Your produce and your wagon now belong to me, farmer. Take your woman and your life and go or you will lose it all."

The mounted men shifted in their saddles. They reminded Tom of cats preparing to play with their prey. Grimacing with pain, Tom removed his hand from the hilt of the sword.

He could barely move his right arm. Tom reached around with his left hand and took hold of the knife. He drew it slowly from his flesh while maintaining eye contact with the red-haired man. When it was free he turned the knife over slowly so that he held it by the blade.

The red-haired man didn't move. He just watched Tom.

With blood pouring from his wound, Tom dismounted and walked over to the wagon. When he got there, he reached up and offered the knife back to the man, "This be yours then."

The man reached down, taking hold of the knife's hilt.

"You have balls, farmer. You have fifteen minutes to leave town on that nag of yours or I'll send these men after you."

Tom nodded. He checked to see if Maggie was breathing. She was unconscious. Blood was coming from her mouth and there was sizeable swelling on the side of her head, but she was alive. They had to leave Marydale within the deadline, but Maggie was not a small woman and now she would be a dead weight. He had to lift her onto his horse with a stiffening and bleeding arm.

The man laughed, "I'd say that you have only ten minutes left, farmer."

Tom hauled Maggie into a sitting position. He would have to lift her onto his shoulders.

Suddenly there was a minor commotion as Barney ran through the cordon of cavalry to be on his knees at Tom's side.

"And who might this be?" said the man.

Tom looked at Barney as he helped guide Maggie onto Tom's good shoulder, "Me boy," he replied.

Without another word, they worked together to get Maggie up across the back of Tom's horse. Then Barney took the reins and led the horse up the road and away from Marydale.

As they passed through the checkpoint, Tom nodded at Barney, "Thank-ee. I am indebted to you, boy."

Barney turned off the road when he heard a short whistle. As he pushed into the undergrowth, Shine and Lucy appeared at their father's side. Together they all passed deeper into the wooded slopes of the forest. Barney noted that Shine's features were marked with several fingernail scratches and bite marks. It appeared that Lucy had been disinclined to wait for his return.

As Barney passed by, Shine caught his eye. For the first time he saw her without her contemptuous façade. She gave him a faint nod and a smile. It took a moment for Barney to realise that she was silently thanking and perhaps praising him. He felt his back straighten with pride. Shine's acknowledgement made him feel a little light-headed.

"That's far enough," said Shine suddenly. Barney stopped the horse beside Shine in a concealed clearing.

While Lucy bound her father's arm to stem the flow of blood and then secured it in a sling, Shine and Barney managed to get Maggie off the horse before gently lowering her to a coarse woollen blanket that they had retrieved from Tom's saddlebag. Maggie groaned. In response, Lucy left her father's side and immediately commenced a thorough inspection of Maggie's wounds.

"Any clean cloth that you can find. Quickly now."

As Barney watched, he saw a side of Lucy that he had never seen before. She worked methodically without rushing. The tip of her tongue poked out of the corner of her mouth as she cleaned the surface of each wound before binding it tightly to slow the bleeding. She hardly spoke as she went about her work other than to give clear instructions to them. She was calm, very, very calm and in her element. No one did anything to distract Lucy's concentration. When Lucy had done all she could, she came over to Shine and Barney.

"Ma has a broken jaw, but that is not the worst of her injuries. I have no way of knowing how her head striking the ground will affect her. I also have no way of treating her properly. I need to reduce the swelling as soon as possible, so I need medicine as well as some fine sharp blades, cord, a needle and clean bandages."

Lucy paused.

"If I can't reduce the swelling, she may be left with an internal injury that will forever dull her brain and inhibit her speech. You see that even now drool pools from the corner of her mouth?"

They all looked at Maggie. Tom, with blood already soaking through his bandage, was by her side tenderly holding her hand.

Barney thought for a moment.

"It's two hours until nightfall. Shine, do you know where to find the Healer in town?"

Shine nodded.

"Lucy, you stay here. There's no one else who can properly care for Maggie and Tom. Make a list of what you need, and we'll fetch everything tonight."

"But they've seen you," said Lucy.

"Only some of them, and they were too busy looking at Tom and Maggie," Barney replied with feigned confidence.

After a short discussion, they decided against building a fire because its light might attract unwanted attention. As all their bedrolls and tents were in the wagon, they spent their time waiting for the daylight to fade constructing an improvised barrier of branches and foliage to prevent the cool breeze that would inevitably blow down from the snow-capped mountains of the northern border from reaching Maggie. Tom was not happy about being excluded from Barney's plan; however, he realised that because of his injury he could be of no use to anyone in Marydale and medical supplies were sorely needed.

After darkness had blackened the forest, Barney and Shine set off, taking care to place sticks in the ground to mark their trail. Soon enough they came to the road, which they followed until they could see Marydale's lights and hear its sounds. They had no desire to risk being challenged by the guards at the checkpoint, so they left the road, pushing through the undergrowth until, once more, they stood beneath the trees.

Frustratingly, no matter how carefully they moved, there was nothing they could do to deaden the noise they created with each footfall. Fallen branches fractured and fallen leaves rustled beneath their feet. They slowed their pace and paused at every foreign noise. It seemed to take forever until they agreed that they had moved beyond the checkpoint's line of sight.

Surprisingly, they saw no light that announced the presence of guards within the tree line. This played on Barney's mind. Then he deduced that the lack of guards was a demonstration of the Duke's confidence that no one was coming to assist the Baron. Considering the matter further, he realised that the encampment that encircled Marydale acted as an effective guard post in its own right. Anyone who approached the town would have to travel through the encampment before they could reach the stores of food and other supplies. While Barney considered the Duke's strategy,

Shine led him to where the tree line was closest to the Healer's home.

They halted beside the ancient trunk of a massive oak tree. From where they stood, at the edge of the tree line, they could see an open grassed area that was bathed in moonlight. Beyond the open area, they could see the first of the campfires and shelters that marked the positions of the Duke's troops. On the other side of the shelters, Marydale appeared to be alive with lights. Barney muttered darkly to himself, wondering if their task would prove to be both impossible and fruitless. There seemed to be no way that they would be able to pass unseen to their destination.

Shine took Barney's hand.

"Any army has its followers. Some are the families of the soldiers. Some are the owners of the supply caravans, and some simply want to be part of events. On this occasion it's even better: some of the folk from Marydale must still live here. Walk slowly and don't act nervous. Act like you belong and have every reason to be here. Don't attempt to hide or pass unseen. Let them see what they want to see: two unthreatening kids who have been in the woods coming home for the night."

Barney swallowed and nodded. He took comfort from Shine's warm hand. He was startled and very distracted by the fact that she was holding it. Without warning, Shine suddenly stepped out from the cover of the trees, dragging him behind her. As they walked, Shine talked loudly about a trip into the hills looking for mushrooms and how her mother would be annoyed that they hadn't been able to find any.

It wasn't long before they passed campfires and rows of tents. Once they were among them, Barney realised that the layout was not random. Most of the shelters were in straightish lines. Common thoroughfares, free from the ropes and pegs that held the shelters in place, led through the encampment. Very few of the troopers glanced at either Shine or Barney. Nearly all of them stayed engrossed in what they were doing; the pair were ignored as if they weren't there.

When they weren't challenged, Barney's confidence grew. He committed to the role that Shine urged him to play and responded to her prompting. Together they wove a tale of foraging for food and hunger. As soon as they mentioned food, they found that they didn't have to act out their hunger; it had been some time since they had eaten and the food being cooked by many of the Duke's troops smelt rather pleasant.

They remained unchallenged as they passed beyond the last of the campfires and into an open area that bordered the village proper: it wasn't long before they were standing on the main street.

Without pause, Shine led Barney straight down one of the side streets to the third house. The house was a wooden two-storey structure with a visible lean to it. It was aged but not old and had a wooden veranda around the outside. Apart from its lean, it appeared to be sturdily built. The ground floor had been divided into a small ward for five or so patients to lie down and recover. The Healer lived upstairs so that he could be close enough to his patients to enable him to properly care for them. That night the Healer was not alone.

The veranda had several men on it. Some were bandaged and immobilised to prevent them from moving and reopening their wounds. Others were gently moaning while they swayed in hammocks that hung from the veranda's rafters.

Shine didn't pause. She walked straight through the open front door and went inside. She dropped Barney's hand the moment she strode through the doorway.

Inside, wounded men were haphazardly lying about. A tall, balding man in a bloodied and stained apron, which had once been white, looked up from where he had been readying his equipment to set a broken arm. He started in surprise at the sight of the two of them. His surprise served to draw the unwanted attention of a menacing trooper who was standing by his side. A mace hung from his belt.

"Who are these two?" the man asked the Healer.

"I... I sent for them. They... they got here far quicker than I thought they would. I n... need assistance."

Turning to Barney and Shine, he said, "Come on you two, I'm paying good coin for your assistance so get stuck in. Don't wait to be told what to do! Shine, move the soiled bandages and bedding outside and set to cleaning them. Boy, come here and hold this man still while I set his arm."

The man with the mace looked at the two who had not moved.

Shine pushed Barney forward and then picked up a pile of soiled linen bandages and bedding.

As Barney approached the Healer, he explained what he needed Barney to do.

"You make Jace right again or youse will regret it," said the man with the mace.

The Healer ignored the man.

The bone in Jace's upper arm had been broken about halfway between his shoulder and his elbow. Barney could see one end of the broken bone pressing against the skin, threatening to break through. Luckily, Jace appeared to be unconscious.

Following the Healer's directions, Barney climbed on the table. He took hold of Jace's upper arm and pinned it against the roll of cloth the Healer had placed along the man's side. When the Healer was satisfied with the limb's position, he bade Barney to bear down with his weight and hold it as tightly as possible. The Healer then took hold of Jace's arm at his elbow, before testing his grip to ensure that he wouldn't slip.

"Hold him still," the Healer said to Barney as he slowly pulled on Jace's elbow.

Barney was fascinated to see the bone move under the surface of Jace's skin. The more the Healer pulled, the tauter the skin on Jace's arm grew. The Healer's effort was obvious from the sweat that beaded on his forehead and from his grunts of exertion.

When the Healer had drawn the lower portion of the broken bone slightly past the break, he slowly and smoothly rotated Jace's elbow until the underside of Jace's forearm was aligned with the underside of Jace's upper arm. Then the Healer gently released some of the pressure to allow the bone to slide back into place. Barney could have sworn that he heard a click just before a look of relief passed over the Healer's face.

The man with the mace looked on with concern as the Healer set a splint along the length of the bone and then bound it tightly to keep it in place.

"I don't know whether there's internal damage. If there is, he might not recover full use of his arm, but the bone will heal," said the Healer.

The man with the mace glowered at the Healer, "I'll come back if it don't heal good and proper!"

Tiring of the man's belligerence, the Healer returned the man's stare with menace, "If you do anything to me, this boy, or my family, I will inform the Captain of the Guard of your actions. We are under his personal protection, as you well know. You'd do well to take your empty threats outside and leave us be. Your friend will be unconscious for some time yet."

The man flexed his hand around the handle of his mace and had to visibly restrain himself as the Healer held his stare. Abruptly he rose and stomped out of the room.

EIGHT

As the front door swung closed, the Healer rounded on Barney and hissed, "The only reason that I have played along is that you were with Shine, and her family means a lot to me. Who are you and what do you want?"

Barney immediately recognised the Healer's need for a full accounting of the truth. As quickly and quietly as he could, he explained his association with Tom and Maggie.

As Barney spoke, he could see the Healer visibly becoming more relaxed. By the time Barney had run through his observations of Maggie's condition and Lucy's list of items, the Healer was sagely nodding his head. When he had nothing further to say, Barney saw no reason to fill the silence. He watched as the Healer thought through what he had been told before he began to pace and fire questions at Barney so that he could gain more knowledge of Maggie's symptoms.

Unfortunately, Barney had no idea whether 'Maggie's eyes had rolled back in her head' or 'the amount of foam within Maggie's drool', or the answer to many other pointed queries. Eventually, the Healer lapsed into silence before announcing that Lucy's course of treatment seemed appropriate.

Barney followed the Healer into a small storeroom beneath the stairs. By the flickering light of a lamp, the Healer took hold of a backpack and began placing the items from Lucy's list into it. The Healer moved with practised ease as he explained that the men in his house, and those in the surrounding village, were part of a much larger body of troops who had marched against the Baron under the Duke's banner.

It was confusing to Barney, whose knowledge of politics had until then been limited to the snippets that his father had passed to him. According to the Healer, the Duke was both the brother and enemy of the King, the Baron was a staunch ally of the King and the Duke had tried to capture the Baron's castle by surprise. However, that attack had failed and the Duke's forces were at that very moment besieging the Baron's castle. Marydale was being used as a rallying point for supplies, reinforcements and treating the wounded.

The Healer could not explain the reason for the Duke's actions or how the siege was progressing. All the Healer knew was that the siege had reached a stalemate after the Duke's initial attack had been repulsed. The Baron still occupied his castle; however, all of Landsend was under the control of the Duke, whose army enforced his will by executing anyone who resisted the occupation.

Most of Marydale's inhabitants, including the Healer's family, had fled when the first of the Duke's troopers arrived. The Healer's leaving had been delayed when he had tried to evacuate his patients with him. Because of the delay, the Healer had been captured and then, once his skills were recognised, he had been forced to treat the Duke's wounded. He stayed, because to leave would have invited the Duke's wrath down upon everyone he had ever cared for. However, in staying and assisting the Duke, the Healer was concerned about what would happen to him and his family if the Baron won the battle. He was worried about how the Baron would react to his assisting the enemy to maintain its fighting force.

Barney reasoned to himself that the Healer was effectively caught between the King's only sibling and the Baron, just like prey between the two sides of a trap.

Barney and the Healer had finished their discussion. The supplies had all been neatly packed into two backpacks, one containing Lucy's medical supplies and the other some blankets, fire-starting equipment, knives, flasks of water and food, when Shine came back through the door. She was carrying a large basket with piles of washed bandages and laundry. She immediately saw that they were seated and sharing a loaf of bread and some sweetmeats and she dropped the basket on the floor.

"So, while I've been out slaving, you've been at your ease, eating and drinking!" Shine spat at Barney.

Barney had forgotten the nature of the task that had been given to Shine and hadn't realised how late it was. He tried smiling, but that made Shine even angrier, so he bowed his head and murmured an apology as he offered her some sweetmeats.

Shine took the food and angrily ate before picking up one of the backpacks and turning to walk out. As she went to leave, she stopped at the door, "Do you know what has become of André?" she asked the Healer.

"I'm sorry, I don't."

Shine's shoulders slumped, "Let's go!"

Barney had no idea who André was, but rather than ask, he hurried to catch up with Shine at the front door. He grabbed her by the shoulder.

"We can't just walk off," he said softly. "Look around you."

There were very few people in the street. Those who were appeared to be patrolling guards or messengers who were up and about doing their masters' bidding. From where Barney and Shine stood, they could see that some of the late-night travellers were being questioned.

It was well after midnight. Leaving the Healer's house wearing backpacks would raise instant suspicion and lead to them being searched. Their backpacks were filled with unusual items and there'd be no easy answers to the questions that would surely be asked. Shine quickly understood Barney's unspoken fear that a search of their persons would mean that they would be detained. It was not going to be easy to slip out of the village. There was simply no excuse for two young people to be travelling alone and towards the woods at night.

They retreated inside, not willing to arouse suspicions by disrupting the rhythm of the military camp.

"We must leave soon," said Shine. "Lucy needs the medicine and we have already been away for too long."

Barney knew that the longer the medical supplies were withheld from Lucy, and the longer Maggie was left untreated, the worse it would be for her. They couldn't afford to spend the night with the Healer, but they also could not walk out into the open.

The Healer recognised their predicament, "The street out the front has the most guards. All the stores are kept in the buildings on the other side of it. You may be challenged in the encampment that encircles Marydale, but while you are passing through it you can act as messengers, servants or tenderers of the fires and just drift between fires or stride as if you are on an errand."

Barney considered this. The Healer went on.

"You should leave by the back door. Behind this house and the next two, there are gardens separated by fences. The gardens are relatively dark because they are generally only used during the day or early evening. You are unlikely to be seen if you go through them, but you'll have to be careful as you are likely to be mistaken as burglars if you are seen."

Barney realised what the Healer had said made sense. They stood a far better chance than walking down the street where they would be questioned. He nodded his agreement.

"Take these two cloaks. Shine, you take one of these staffs. I recall seeing you practising with one at your farm. It may assist you."

Barney and Shine thanked the Healer for his help as they donned the dark cloaks. They noted with satisfaction that they had hoods that they could pull over their heads. These hoods would hide their faces in shadows. Shine accepted one of the stout staffs, choosing one about three-quarters her height. She hefted it to test its weight in her hands before they left.

"Come with us," Barney said to the Healer, as he paused at the threshold of the door.

"They will hardly miss you, but if I go missing, they will search all the surrounding area and my family is out there somewhere. They would put my wife and any of my other family members to the sword if they found them. I thank you for the offer, but it would be too dangerous for you to be with me."

Barney saw that Shine was motioning to him from the rear of the garden. Her outline was indistinct, making it difficult to see her, but he could almost feel her annoyance rippling towards him despite the distance between them. Barney hurriedly thanked the Healer and took his leave, hurrying to where Shine was impatiently waiting. As he approached, Shine took off along the back fence of the garden without speaking a word.

Looking back, the pair watched as the Healer softly shut the door behind him. They followed his progress upstairs by his swaying lantern. The Healer was silhouetted briefly against the upstairs window as he leant out to close the shutters. Once they were closed, Barney and Shine felt very alone.

It took a moment for Barney and Shine's eyes to fully adjust to the darkness. No light intruded into the gardens from inside the two homes on their path. Beyond the rear fence of the Healer's garden, the dwellings appeared to be dark and unwelcoming. Satisfied that no one was watching, Barney and Shine approached the first of the three fences.

They discovered that a hedge, which was bereft of recent care, bounded the Healer's yard. Together, they managed to push aside the foliage to open a gap, which they pushed through without too much trouble, bar a few scratches.

The yard that they entered was dark and filled with shadows. It was dominated by a chicken coop. They edged slowly away from it and closer to the house to avoid disturbing the proud rooster who slept in the midst of his hens. They passed unseen towards the second fence.

The second fence was wooden, and most of it was showing signs of age. Vertical palings were fixed to horizontal bars on the other side of the fence, and the bars were held in place by vertical poles. Between each paling there were gaps of varying widths that had been created by the shrinkage of the wood over time.

Barney tested a few of the palings nearest the house, noting that some of them appeared to be new. He pointed back down along the fence towards the chicken coop. Hopefully, they would have better luck further away from the house. They moved as silently as they could back down the fence, checking for any loose palings as they went. Finally, Barney pointed at a gap between two of the older-looking palings and then to Shine's staff.

Shine nodded in response.

Working together, they inserted the tip of Shine's staff through the gap. When the staff was in place, they worked their way down its shaft towards the other end before glancing around. Seeing nothing untoward, they pushed the staff towards the fence. At first, despite their combined weight, the paling refused to budge. They continued to exert constant pressure on the staff until the paling was levered away from its fellows. It dragged with it some of the nails that had fixed it in place. The nails were obviously old. Some snapped easily and others, eroded by rust, pulled away. The paling groaned but made very little noise as it shifted towards them.

Repeating the process, they inserted the tip of the staff between the next two palings. Once again they pushed on the staff to try to pry the paling towards them. The paling moved slightly but then refused to give any further. They applied more weight; the staff and the paling bowed. Suddenly, the paling gave way, snapping in half. Such was the force that they were applying to the staff that they could do nothing to prevent their fingers being squashed between the fence and the staff. It was as if they had forcibly punched the fence.

The snapping of the paling and the noise of their knuckles hitting the fence awoke one of the chickens who squawked in alarm. A dog that had been asleep in the house took up the alarm and immediately commenced to bark. She was not sure what she was barking at but nevertheless, she barked to alert her owner that something was amiss.

The red-haired owner of the dog leant over his bed, took hold of his boot and opened his eyes just wide enough to see the animal near the closed bedroom door. He hurled his boot at the dog, hitting it in its side.

"Shut up, you mangy animal!"

The dog yelped and then sat silently with ears raised, listening for any further noise.

The Captain of the Guard fell back to sleep, certain that no one would dare attempt to steal either his chickens or his eggs.

Outside, Barney and Shine stood frozen to the spot, nursing their injured knuckles. They stared at each other as they listened, first to the dog, followed by the owner's command and then to the silence. The hen sleepily clucked again before returning to sleep. The rooster opened his eyes and peered into the darkness, seeking out any threat. He paced along the boundary of the coop. Nothing appeared to be amiss. Barney and Shine tried their best to shrink into their cloaks. Seeing nothing, the rooster checked on each of his hens before settling back down.

Barney motioned to Shine to go through the hole they had made into the third garden. He followed as quickly as he could. When he was through, he allowed himself a brief moment to nurse his swelling knuckles before following Shine's lead to the third and final fence.

The last fence was similar to the second one, but this time they couldn't lever the palings aside as the horizontal support was facing them; instead, after a whispered discussion, they decided to climb over it as quickly as possible.

"I'll go first," whispered Shine, "I'm taller than you. Push me up to the top and then I'll reach down and help you over."

Barney nodded and cupped his hands so that Shine could step into them. Springing up, Shine caught hold of the top of the fence and as Barney pushed on the soles of her shoes, she pulled herself up and manoeuvred her body until she was sitting on the fence facing towards him.

"Reach towards me with the staff and I will try pulling you up."

Barney reached up with the staff and Shine grasped it firmly. As soon as she pulled on the staff, Barney's shoulder felt as if it had been lanced with a blade. With a yelp, he let go.

Letting go was the worst thing for Shine. She had braced her body to prevent herself from being pulled forward; however, she had done nothing to prevent herself from falling backwards, so when Barney's weight was suddenly and unexpectedly released, she dropped the staff as she tumbled backwards off the fence before falling to the ground.

"Well, what do we have here then?" growled a voice.

Shine looked up. She had fallen awkwardly on her back, winding herself, and was now looking up into the face of the man with the mace from the Healer's house.

The man reached down and picked Shine up by the front of her cloak, lifting her so that her feet were no longer on the ground. He pushed her against the fence.

Barney couldn't see what was happening, but he heard enough to know that something was amiss.

Looking around, he saw a chair on the veranda of the house. Sprinting to the veranda, he picked up the chair and raced with it back to the fence. He set it against the palings and then threw the staff over the fence. Taking fifteen steps back, he ran and launched himself from the back of the chair at the fence.

It was one of the most ungainly attempts that Barney would ever make at climbing; however, it was successful. His leap succeeded in bringing him to chest height against the fence, which meant that he no longer had to pull himself up but rather could push himself up and over the fence.

Barney held himself in place for a few seconds before he toppled over the fence where, but for his hands reacting on instinct, he would have landed on his head. Sprawled on the ground, he saw the man holding Shine look around.

Shine took advantage of the distraction and kneed the man in his groin before slapping him across his face, but all the man did was laugh, lift her higher and throw her to the ground beside Barney.

Barney crouched, sprang and threw himself at the man's legs.

The man didn't appear to feel a thing. He leant down and picked up Barney by his legs, breaking Barney's grip on his own. He lifted him until Barney's torso was in line with his face.

What he hadn't noticed was that Shine was also on her feet and that she had armed herself with her staff. Grasping it with two hands, she lifted it, without finesse, high above her head before swinging it back down with all the force she could muster onto the back of the man's head, knocking him out cold. Still holding Barney's legs, the man fell forward on top of Barney. Barney was squashed beneath the man's stomach, with the man's head resting on the ground between Barney's legs.

The sound of the scuffle had not gone unnoticed. A patrol raised the alarm. "Run," shouted Shine and she sped off through the first of the tents towards the trees.

The Captain of the Guard's dog vocalised the alarm, throwing herself at the door of her master's room.

Barney wriggled and squirmed before finally managing to twist and squeeze himself out from beneath the prone form.

He pushed himself to his feet.

"You there. Halt!"

Barney propelled himself forward, sprinting towards the lines of tents.

"I said halt!"

An arrow passed over his shoulder, so close to his ear that he could have sworn its flight grazed his cheek.

Barney swerved to his left, crossing the path of the arrow. He had chosen correctly. Instinctively, he should have moved away from the arrow, and the archer had adjusted his aim accordingly. A second arrow passed to his right.

Barney was amongst the first line of tents now. With his head down and arms pumping, he was aware that sleepy soldiers were emerging from their tents. Some were bare-chested and dishevelled from being awoken from a deep sleep. All were armed.

In front of him his path was blocked by a soldier who was crouched with arms spread wide.

Barney had just enough control of his flight to step off his right foot. The soldier was left grasping at air.

Barney was now dangerously unbalanced. With flailing arms, he found himself heading directly towards a firepit that had been used to cook an evening meal. He was running straight at the boundary stones that were set about the cooling coals with no ability to change direction. The metal tripod that had held a stew pot was still in place.

Barney leapt. As he soared, he attempted to brush the tripod to one side. Twisting in the air, he became hopelessly entangled. One of his boots sank into the surface of the firepit. His torso struck the tripod. Its surface had looked deceptively dark and cool, but there were still hot coals beneath the surface. He could feel the heat envelop his boot.

His momentum carried him beyond the boundary of the firepit and he fell, sprawling on his chest.

Bracing his hands against the earth, he tried to push himself to his feet. A large foot struck him squarely on his backpack, directly between his shoulder blades, driving him back to the ground. The weight of an adult trooper was transferred to his back. "Stay!"

Barney tried to squirm sideways. The tip of a sword was rested upon his cheek. It was sharp enough to cause a thin red line of blood to appear, "I said – stay!" The foot pushed down with more force.

Barney had no option but to comply. He was trapped.

When he had ceased to struggle long enough to satisfy his captor, a hand gripped his hair and he was hauled to his feet. He looked about in desperation but realised that he was encircled. Slowly, he raised his hands in a gesture of surrender. More soldiers gathered about him, and any hopes of escape were quickly dashed.

"Out of my way!"

The crowd parted and through it stepped the bare-chested, red-haired Captain of the Guard, his snarling dog trotting beside him.

Barney again looked for a way to escape, but it was evident that there was none.

The Captain looked him over, "The farmer's boy, or should I now call you the fire walker?" He smirked. "Search him."

Barney's backpack was immediately taken from him and emptied. Blankets, food, knives and fire-starting equipment tumbled to the ground.

"So, how did you come by these?"

"Stole them."

The Captain glowered at him. "Why?"

"My ma, that you hit, needs help and all our stuff was in the wagon that you stole." Barney was glad that Shine had the backpack with the medical supplies.

The Captain looked him over, "I'm not sure whether you, boy, have bigger balls than your father. You come unarmed into our camp and steal from us?"

The men around Barney responded with an ugly laugh.

"I take it that the girl was your sister?"

Barney stayed quiet. There was no point in further antagonising the man.

"We punish thieves with death, boy. Did you know that?"

The dog by the Captain's side growled. She still remembered the sting of the boot that had been flung at her and she blamed this man-child.

"Just wanted to help me ma," said Barney, standing straight and tall before the Captain.

"No grovelling for me to take pity? It's lucky for us that the Baron doesn't have more men like you." Some of the surrounding soldiers laughed mirthlessly.

Glancing down at his dog, the Captain grinned evilly.

"Well lads, are you up for some sport? I say give the supplies back to the boy, take his knives and then we give him a head start. I'll bet ten silvers that my dog takes him down before the edge of the forest."

Immediately, the mood of the men changed; the backpack was refilled and thrust back into Barney's hands, and then he was appraised as though he was some animal on show. The length of the head start, and his odds of making the trees were debated and settled without anyone asking Barney's opinion. Eventually, it was settled that the flight of two javelin throws would be used to determine the length of Barney's head start and that should he make the tree line and touch the trunk of a tree, the Captain would call his dog back. Apparently, this would give Barney both a fighting chance and sufficient incentive to make a spectacle of the hunt. Grimly, Barney noted that his chances were so 'good' that no one was placing any money on him making it to the trees; the only money was on how far he would make it.

Despite the time, some fifty men had gathered around Barney. When all bets were placed, they opened a corridor through which he could see the trees beckoning to him beyond the encampment.

A man with two long javelins presented himself to the Captain. It was his job to throw each javelin from a ten-step run. When the second javelin hit the ground, the dog would be released.

Barney's cloak was torn from him, wiped across his bloodied cheek and given to the dog to smell. She was already snarling in anticipation of the hunt when the Captain turned to ensure she was ready. One look at the way she held herself, her whole body pointed at her quarry with muscles quivering with anticipation of being released, and he knew that all she needed was his command.

"Boy. Make ready. Run!"

Barney was thrust forward. He stumbled the first few steps. The man with the javelin was already well into his run and before Barney knew it, the first javelin was launched to the sounds of the cheering men.

Barney gathered his feet under him and then, when he had regained his balance, he ran forward, bursting from the corridor of men. As he ran, he glanced to his left and right, looking for anything that he could use. Stumbling, turning, searching, he ran on. Nothing useful presented itself.

Far ahead of him the first javelin had reached the apex of its flight path and was dipping towards the ground. It would land far to his right and away from the tree line.

On and on he ran, hurtling through one end of a large open tent and out the other. The first javelin embedded itself in the ground to the cheers of the men behind him. In that split second, Barney made a decision. Instead of continuing to run straight for the trees, he turned behind a tent and sprinted towards where the javelin was now embedded in the ground.

Behind him, Barney heard another roar from the onlookers. Either they approved of his will to fight for his life, or the second javelin had been launched. Barney wasn't sure what they were cheering for.

The Captain, understanding Barney's tactic, beckoned an archer to come to him.

"A silver if you can prevent the boy from reaching the javelin."

Barney was now running across the lines of tents. The spaces were confined, and the guy ropes were far more frequent. He was two-thirds of the way to the javelin when an arrow thudded into the ground to his right. More arrows followed, but for a short time Barney knew he had the advantage. Before they shot, his enemy had to be sure that they would not hit one of their own and the narrow corridors through which he fled provided a degree of cover. With little ability to deviate from his path, and no real choice, he decided to ignore the arrows. He had no time to waste and the risk of injury from an arrow was, in the circumstances, inconsequential when weighed against the certainty of a horrifying death if the dog caught him.

Behind him he heard another cheer as the second javelin hit the ground and the dog was freed. Now the race was on. More wagers were placed on whether Barney would reach his intended goal. At that moment Barney wished for Lucy's speed.

Barney could hear the dog now, a feral rumble of anger in full flight after him. The troopers were right; he would never have made the trees.

Rounding a tent, he caught sight of the javelin. He was within a body length of it when the dog rounded the same tent. In two paces the dog tensed to leap, aiming to land on Barney's back.

Barney dived beneath the angled shaft of the javelin.

The dog leapt.

Barney had no time to pluck the javelin from the ground or turn to face the dog. With his heart pounding, he made a leap of faith to believe in logic. He knew that the dog was in the air, and he believed that the dog's target would be his back. It was the largest, most exposed surface of the animal's prey. With his back still towards the dog, he slid on his knees beneath the javelin. Leaving the point embedded in the ground, he pulled the javelin down so that it was braced on his shoulder and angled back to where the centre of his back had been but moments before.

Barney was either lucky or brilliant, or perhaps a little of both. The dog realised the danger in mid-flight and attempted to contort her body in the air, but there was no way that she could change direction. The full force of her body fell on the butt of the javelin. The weapon pierced the animal's chest and, for a brief moment, the animal was held in the air directly above and behind Barney.

Howling in pain, the dog's front paws came to rest on Barney's back, and she scratched at his backpack, but her broken rib and punctured lung together with the presence of the foreign object in her body were enough to stall the ferocity of the attack.

Barney let go of the javelin's shaft and scampered away.

Glancing back, Barney noted that the javelin remained embedded in the dog as she backed off, snarling, trailing the javelin behind her. She was obviously in great distress.

Sucking in a deep breath, Barney rose and this time he ran straight for the tree line.

Behind him, the men were cheering in enjoyment of their sport. Angry at the mortal wound to one of his beloved dogs, the Captain snatched the bow and the quiver of arrows from the archer.

The Captain's first shot found the dog and silenced her forever. Then he aimed at Barney.

Fear spurred Barney's feet, but once again he found enough time between ragged breaths to think. As randomly as he could he sidestepped and ran in diagonal lines, rather than straight towards the trees. An arrow passed through the space to his right where he had been just a moment before and then another to his left.

The Captain now realised that the boy might make the trees. He ordered a mounted member of the camp's guard to pursue the boy. The Captain shot another arrow at Barney who appeared to cleverly dive out of its way at the last moment. The onlookers had no way of knowing that Barney had tripped over a protruding tree root that his tired legs had refused to leap over.

Barney was close to the trees now, but he could hear the horse. Putting his head down, he ran on.

The horse was between Barney and the Captain. The Captain no longer had a line of sight. In anger he snapped the bow over his knee and cast the pieces aside.

Barney reached the tree line and thrust his left hand onto the nearest tree before turning around to face towards the spectators. He could see a cantering horse closing the distance and beyond that, the group of men who had been betting on his fate. In a desperate attempt to gain their favour, he waved at the onlookers with his right hand. When he was sure that he had their attention, he flourished his right hand above his head and bowed.

The horse was closer now.

Barney's actions resulted in a massive cheer and laughter from the men. The Captain could either allow the pursuit of the horseman to continue or honour the terms of the bet. His men would accept either ending as, although the sport had pleased them, it was over. He contemplated his position and then, despite the fact that one of his beloved dogs was dead, he acknowledged to himself that he would be remembered more for honouring the bet than killing the boy.

He gritted his teeth. Well lad, you can avoid being killed, but you cannot avoid death itself.

Raising his arm, the Captain communicated his intentions to the horseman, who had indecisively slowed his horse when Barney had stopped at the tree. The confused rider, who was not privy to the terms of the bet, reined in his mount.

Barney bowed again to the cheering men who clearly approved of the way the events had unfolded. Then, before anything further could happen, he turned and forced himself to walk slowly into the trees.

When the foliage was dense enough to hide him from sight, Barney stopped, fell to his knees and threw up. He was still vomiting when he heard his name being called. Suddenly Shine was there beside him. She held him tightly until his convulsions ceased and his body stopped shaking.

◆

As Barney fought to tame his breathing and shaking, Shine repeatedly apologised for not freeing him from beneath the guard's weight. Finally, when Barney had sufficiently recovered, they set off in what they believed to be the general direction of the road.

Barney and Shine were unable to follow a straight line due to the densely packed tree trunks. The lack of distinguishable landmarks, coupled with the darkness that enveloped them, made it impossible for them to navigate with certainty. Uncertainty led to guesswork and before long they were disorientated and lost. They squabbled with increasing frequency and it was only through luck, and after what seemed an eternity, that they stumbled into a glade where the canopy of the trees opened to the night sky.

From the centre of the clearing, Shine stopped and pointed, "I told you over and over that we were going the wrong way, but you wouldn't listen. There are no other settlements in the area. That light is coming from Marydale!"

Barney glowered but bit his lip. Under the trees they had both been bereft of any sense of direction for some time. There was no way that either he or Shine could tell where Marydale was. She was right about the lights. They could only point to Marydale's location and they were to their right and not to their left. They had been travelling in the opposite direction to the one they had intended.

Barney took a deep breath. He realised that they were tired and annoyed with both themselves and each other. It was pointless to argue. They had more than likely doubled the time that it would take to make their way back to Lucy, Maggie and Tom and there was no telling whether the delay would have dire consequences for Maggie.

Barney stared at the night sky without responding to Shine, who was still staring at him waiting for a reaction. If they simply stepped back under the canopy they would have no visible reference points. They would risk wandering, once again, from their intended path.

"We need to return to Marydale and then use it to find the road."

"No – really. You don't say. And how are we supposed to find Marydale in the dark? We couldn't even find the road."

"We take turns to climb as we go. One of us will climb as high as it takes to where we can see the light leaking into the night sky above Marydale."

"You want me to climb?"

"Yes. I won't be able to do it all. My shoulder wouldn't cope. Unless you think that you couldn't manage it."

"Of course, I can climb," Shine responded with all the justifiable haughtiness that she could muster.

Their travel was tedious and tiring. It was not until after the moon had set that Marydale itself came into sight. The village had returned to normal. The excitement of Barney's escape had been forgotten. Even though they were anxious to be away from the village, Barney and Shine stayed just within the tree line, keeping the encampment in sight. It didn't take as long as Barney had expected before they pushed through undergrowth to find the road before them. They gratefully followed it until they came to the path that they had marked out.

This time, travelling through the forest was easier. They were exhausted and stumbling over their own leaden feet, but they remembered to pull out each marker to hide their path. It was only when they realised that there were no more markers to follow that they realised they had reached their destination: the clearing where they had left Lucy, Maggie and Tom. It now stood empty. If it wasn't for the remnants of the shelter that they had hastily constructed for Maggie, they would have convinced themselves that they were in the wrong place.

The dappled early morning light, coupled with their lack of rest, inhibited their ability to focus so neither Barney nor Shine could find any sign of tracks leading from the clearing. Their search became increasingly frantic. Their fears were magnified by their sleep-deprived state and they moved hurriedly, without attempting to conduct a methodical search. They searched and then re-searched the same areas looking for anything that made sense. They found no clues. Eventually, as self-doubt crept in, they bickered about whether they were in the correct spot and how there should be some sign of what had occurred.

"We took too long to return and now they are gone. Come on, let's go. They'll have been taken back to Marydale," said Barney glumly.

As they turned to leave, a short, shadowy figure stepped into their path.

Barney leapt back. Shine readied her staff.

"You two argue more than two cats fighting over a bird," said the shadow gruffly.

The hood of the cloak that obscured the man's features slid back to reveal his face. He could have been no more than five foot tall.

"I have been sitting here, at the foot of this tree, waiting for one of you to find me. Looks like you are both blind to what is in front of you. You're blinded by what you expect to see and what you want to see."

The man made no effort to draw any weapon, holding out both of his hands palm up to show that he was unarmed.

"Who are you?" asked Barney.

"He's a trapper who often visits Marydale; I believe his name is Bertrand," said Shine, as she relaxed both her stance and her grip on her staff.

"He's a midget with attitude," mumbled Barney flatly under his breath.

"At your service, m'lady," said Bertrand with a flourishing bow. He ignored Barney.

"Where are our friends?" asked Barney.

"In a safe place. Come along. Follow me."

Without another word, Bertrand set off, leaving them with no option other than to follow him. It was easy to follow Bertrand now that he wasn't wearing his hood. Previously, it had served to create indistinct shadows about his head. Despite his mood, Barney found that he grudgingly admired how silently Bertrand moved over the forest floor. He seemed to barely disturb any of the leaf litter.

They travelled for over an hour as the light from the rising sun filtered down through the leaves and onto the forest floor. Eventually, they found themselves passing a bubbling spring whose waters led them to the entrance of the narrowest of valleys. After a time, the waters of the spring were fed from other sources, and it wasn't long before they found themselves walking beside a shallow stream which playfully trickled over a stony riverbed. Over time, as the layer of soil from the riverbed had been washed away, the rocks had been able to disturb and direct the water's flow, challenging it to change course. Small ponds had formed beside the main flow in the softer ground beside the stream, causing the breadth of the watercourse to gradually broaden.

Barney was so tired that he could barely walk, let alone think, when two men leapt into their path with swords drawn. Barney jumped back in fright. As he did, he tripped and fell – landing on his backside in the water.

"Heard you that time, Bertrand. Those two sound like blind oxen blundering along," said one of the men between chuckles.

Bertrand, ignoring Barney's plight, returned the friendly greeting, "These are the last of that party that I brought in earlier. No one else is meant to be following. Keep an eye out."

The men nodded in response and let them proceed without any further interruption.

They ducked down to push beneath bushes whose limbs gently caressed the waters of the stream. Beyond the bushes the riverbank widened to accommodate a collection of tents and makeshift shelters. Barney estimated that the camp was occupied by around fifty to sixty people. From the temporary nature of the structures, it was fairly evident that the occupants of the camp were refugees from the damage and destruction that was being wrought by Duke Jacoby's army.

Bertrand led the companions to a large tent that was on one side of the encampment. When they entered, they found themselves standing before straw pallets, most of which were occupied by the sick and injured. Lucy was standing in the middle of the tent. She was surrounded by the attendants of the sick and from the way she was being addressed, Lucy had clearly taken charge.

Shine placed a restraining hand on Barney. "Let her finish. She will have already treated Ma and she'll realise that we're here soon enough."

All Barney wanted to do was get out of his wet trousers. He fidgeted while Lucy kept gesturing at the beds of the patients around her. It was difficult for Barney to pinpoint why Lucy, despite her youthfulness, had everyone's respect. Perhaps it was the direct answers that she gave to their questions or maybe it was the element of confidence that Barney had never seen in her before. Whatever the reason, Lucy was holding everyone's attention and respect.

Finally, when the last of her attendants had scurried off on their designated tasks, Lucy beckoned for them to come to her. They wound their way around several beds and once they were in reach, she hugged them both tightly.

"You had me worried. Don't do that again – either of you. Now, were you successful?"

Barney nodded and Lucy's face immediately lit up.

Barney and Shine removed their backpacks and offered them to Lucy. She opened the flaps of the packs and rummaged around inside of them, humming a happy tune before looking up.

"Well done. We'll catch up later. They've run out of a few things here so I'll prepare these for Ma. Be off with you both. You look like the living dead. Find somewhere to sleep."

Barney slumped outside, shuffled beneath the shade of a nearby tree, forgot about his wet trousers, lay down and immediately fell into a deep and dreamless sleep. He was unaware that Shine followed him and curled herself into a ball near his head. When Lucy found Barney and gently tucked a blanket around his prone body, he felt nothing.

For a week while Shine, Barney and Tom assisted in the gathering of food and attended to the many other tasks needed to run the camp, Maggie lay still, barely seeming to breathe. Lucy was a fixture by her side. She used every ounce of her skill to care for her mother.

Late in the evening of the eighth day, an exhausted Lucy found Barney exercising his shoulder.

"Ma is awake, and she wants to see you."

The tent in which Maggie lay was simple but warm and clean. She lay propped up in her bed with a pillow behind her back, gingerly sipping watery soup from a spoon that Shine held patiently to her lips. The left side of her face seemed to be heavier than the right and her lips didn't seem to be able to seal sufficiently to keep the liquid in. Shine spent as much time wiping her mother's chin as she did spooning soup into her mouth.

When Maggie saw Barney, she motioned for Shine to stop. She clearly struggled to think of the words that she wanted to say and her parched and cracked lips, swollen throat and broken jaw created difficulties for her.

"Thank ye... go to your mother... tell her... about... yer father."

Barney nodded. He had been wanting to go from the moment that he had delivered the medical supplies to Lucy, but it just hadn't felt right. Before he could respond, Lucy, with tears in her eyes, took his hand and led him to the door and virtually pushed him outside, "Don't distress her. Go now. She needs her rest."

Outside, Barney literally bumped into Tom.

"So, you're off then?"

"Yes."

Tom handed him a knife that was as long as Barney's forearm, "You'll be needing this."

"And I'm going with him," said a voice from behind Barney.

Tom started. "No Shine. The boy goes alone. I'll be needing ya to help care for yer mother."

"No, Father. I am no farmer and no healer. You've told me that many times. André will need someone to guide him here –"

"Not that boy again. André is not for you and the boy's issues are not yours. I refuse permission for you to go."

Shine glowered at her father; her eyebrows raised and her pupils became tiny points of black and her face went beetroot red as the volume of her voice dropped to barely a whisper, "Da, I have never said no to you before, but in this, you will not deny me. I. Will. Go!"

Tom and Shine stared directly into each other's eyes as if each could force the other to back down merely through force of their will. Barney watched as an entire gamut of emotion passed through Tom: red hot anger, denial, bereavement and finally acceptance. Without a word, he pushed past Barney and Shine and opened the tent flap before letting it snap shut behind him.

As the flap closed, Shine collapsed on the ground, but when Barney went to help her up, she pushed him away.

"Leave me. Be ready at first light," she said. With that, she stood up and walked away from him.

C H A P T E R

TEN

—— ✦ ——

The following morning, before the light of the sun challenged the light of the lamps and candles adorning the shelter in which he rested, Barney was shaken awake by Shine.

"Time to move. Bertrand is going to act as our guide," she whispered as she thrust some bread dripping with honey into his hand.

Barney swung his legs over the side of his bed and laced up his boots as he wolfed down his breakfast. When he was ready, he slipped quietly outside, making sure not to wake any of the people scattered around him. He found Lucy waiting for him. She returned his backpack and gave him a series of rapid instructions about the lotions and supplies that she had packed for him before giving him a beaming smile and a hug for good luck.

Bertrand stood nearby. When he decided they were ready to go, he turned and started walking, obviously expecting that they would follow him.

Barney had to hurry to catch up; he realised that he had not thanked Lucy, but he had no time even to turn to wave. Shine paced behind Bertrand, using her staff as a walking stick.

They followed the stream for most of the morning before Bertrand turned away from it.

They travelled slowly but steadily in a circuitous route through the forest towards Landsend, taking regular but short breaks. The trees that they passed were a canvas for all sorts of moss and fungi. At times, the ground squirmed with leeches that sought their flesh. Everything smelt and felt damp. The denseness of the trees made Barney and Shine feel insignificant, especially as neither of them had ever been so far from the beaten track. They heard very few sounds, apart from the occasional bird. Even then, their noise was muted. The air felt oppressive and heavy enough to weigh down everything. It seemed as though the forest resented them making any sound to mark their passing so there was little conversation.

Finally, after a full day of travel, the trees began to thin out, and a breeze tainted with the smell of smoke plucked at their hair and cooled the sweat on their skin. Before long, they could see the blue sky smeared with black smoke through the canopy of trees. The smoke became more distinct as they followed its path towards the Baron's castle.

The castle was located on a low rise roughly at the centre of a natural basin valley that had only two points of access for carts and wagons. The Northern Road, which was guarded by a series of towers, forts and walls that were manned by those unfortunate enough to be conscripted into the King's army, wound its way down from the border, through the Black Gate on the far side of the valley, and on to the castle. The Southern Road made its way down from the Baron's castle towards Marydale and then on to the other five counties of the Kingdom.

The valley itself looked as though it had been carved from some long-forgotten impact. The effect of the impact, although still readily apparent, had weathered over time so that parts of the tall cliffs that had once encircled the valley had been worn away to create steep grassy slopes, which the more adventurous sledded down in winter.

These weathered slopes were lined with the trees of the ever-present forest that stood sentry-like and teetered along the ridge. The trees had always given Barney the impression that they were willing, at any moment, to flow down in a great tsunami of green onto the valley floor. To the north, peaks of a mountain range were forever dusted with snow.

The location of the castle and its need for supplies had forever changed the surrounding area. The best of the fertile and accessible ground had been cleared so that farms could grow produce for the castle. Small farm holdings now dotted the landscape and communities such as Marydale had sprung up to meet the needs of the rural community. In turn, those communities had driven the need for more provisions and people. Over time, the importance of the castle and the township that nestled about its walls had grown until it had developed into the central trade and communication hub for the county. With the construction of the Wall, the importance of the county had been recognised through the appointment of its first baron. This had given the population even more reason to grow. The populace that supported the castle belonged to the most northern town of the Kingdom, which they had begun calling "Landsend", as it was quite literally the last town before the end of the Kingdom's land.

Over the years, several thousand people had come to live in Landsend. At first, the township had grown haphazardly when guardsmen, whose job it was to defend the castle, had erected shelters for their families close to the castle's walls. This inner circle now formed what was known as "Old Town". As more people came to settle around the castle, different and well-ordered districts of trade, smithies, stable yards and taverns had grown without any overarching plan.

Several decades ago, Baron Aethelson's great-grandfather had determined that he wanted Landsend to be more ordered and had attempted to replace the older buildings in Old Town. That baron had never accomplished this task and had only managed to replace the dwellings and shops that stood along the avenue leading to the castle's main entrance. Beyond those new buildings, the ramshackle houses and the narrow twisting avenues of Old Town had continued to thrive, with all the vibrancy of a tight-knit community whose generations had grown up together.

Now, from where the trio lay on their bellies amongst wildflowers, clumps of various grasses and vines on the valley's rim, they could see a township that was very different to what any of them remembered or imagined.

On the outer reaches of Landsend, groups of houses and businesses had been razed to the ground. In their place, stood vast catapults that were launching rocks and burning pitch high into the air. These loads were meant to fall on, or over, the walls of the castle, but they occasionally fell short and landed in Old Town, haphazardly destroying anything in their path.

Those within the castle were firing back as best they could. In turn, their missiles fell, with the same degree of accuracy, on the attacking forces. The castle wall's base was blackened. In many places, birds of prey were circling and landing, confirming that carrion had collected at the foot of the castle wall, presumably because of the Duke's attacks upon it.

Baron Aethelson's flag hung limply from the castle's central tower, indicating that the castle was still in his hands. The companions could see movement along the battlements that marked the presence of some of the defenders of the castle.

It seemed that the tales the Healer had passed on to Barney were correct. Landsend gave every appearance of being firmly in the hands of the Duke. They could see rallying points for the Duke's troops throughout the town and his troops entered and exited its streets confidently, without any sign that they expected to be attacked.

Bertrand looked at the companions.

"I can go no further," Bertrand said. "I will wait for you for three full days from tomorrow morning. If you do not come back to me in that time, I will return to the camp without you. You should observe the patrols before you try to enter the town. Late tonight, after the moon has set, would be a good time to try. Don't go near their siege engines as they will be closely guarded; enter where their patrols are the thinnest."

Barney nodded his thanks to Bertrand. They shimmied away from their observation post. For Tom's sake Barney decided to make one last appeal to Shine, "You don't have to come with me. Maggie needs– "

Shine tersely interrupted, "You won't stop me."

Barney sighed, "Who is this André anyway and where will we find him?"

"André is... someone I know well. He's a friend who's always been there for me. He'll be inside the town, somewhere in the traders' section, unless he has been able to escape..."

"Where in the traders' section?"

"His family traded in dyed cloth. I've never been there. I've only ever managed to meet him in Marydale."

Barney had been to the dye merchants' streets. He vividly remembered the stench and the shouting of the merchants as they hawked their wares. In his mind, he mapped out Landsend, following the route from his home, through the stable yards, through the streets lined with taverns and then to the outer reaches of the town where the cloth merchants had been located.

He pointed. "We will have to go round this valley following the tree line to the left until we are about halfway around. From there we can enter the markets and the merchants' quarter. Do you have any idea where he actually lives? We'll go there first. From there we can go to my home, which is in Old Town below the castle walls."

"Can you get me to the main cloth market?"

"Yes."

"André has explained to me how I can find his family's shop from the cloth market, just in case I could ever convince my father to allow me to visit."

Barney nodded. Bertrand, seeing that Shine wouldn't be coming with him, took his leave. The die was cast.

ELEVEN

F rom experience, Barney knew that if they stayed just within the trees they could not be seen from Landsend, so, unless sentries had been posted in the forest, they would not be spotted. He surmised that it was highly unlikely for sentries to be in the forest as there was only one road for any reinforcements and it led directly through Marydale.

Their trip was, just as Barney had hoped, uneventful. No permanent sentries had been stationed in the forest although they did come across evidence of patrols having been through the area. When they reached what Barney determined to be the best location to enter the town, they used the moonlight to spy on the town's defences.

A ring of evenly spaced campfires lay between them and the outskirts of the town. Around each of the campfires there were at least three sentries who were sitting and cooking their evening meal. A sentry stood on either side of the outer rim of the light generated by the campfires. They could also see another sentry standing between the town's outskirts and each of the campfires, facing in. The positioning of the sentries meant that their night vision would be largely unaffected by the glow of the fire, and they could see anyone attempting to escape the town and anyone trying to enter it. The position of the sentries nearest the town gave Barney the strong impression that the Duke had allocated more resources to monitoring those who were attempting to leave the encircled township than preventing anyone from entering it. It was also evident that there were no handy stands of bushes, creeks or any substantive cover between where they were and the town.

The guards at the campfires did not appear to be ill-disciplined in any way. They were not drinking or gambling. Indeed, those at the closest campfire looked like friends on a camping trip, occasionally laughing and talking as they cooked what looked like a small, skinned rabbit over an open fire.

As they watched, Barney and Shine chewed on some cold dried meat.

After the guards around the fire had eaten, all three of them stood and replaced those who had been on active duty so that they could eat their meal.

Shine sat with her back resting against the trunk of a nearby tree, "Wake me when you're tired or if you find a way in."

Barney nodded and turned back to watch the sentries.

It was well after midnight when Barney shook Shine awake.

"Quickly. Move."

By the time Shine had stood, Barney was already disappearing through the last of the trees. Shine rushed to catch up with him.

Barely able to keep their balance, they sprinted down the steep slope with windmilling arms. Several times they came close to falling head over heels.

When Shine had the chance, she looked up and understood why Barney had chosen that moment to rush towards the town without attempting to take cover. A large group of people were running from the town and the sentries were converging on the escapees to try to intercept them. A running skirmish had developed. For the moment, the attention of all the sentries was focussed on the escaping townsfolk.

Wooden and steel bars, knives and improvised weapons were met with swords and arrows. To Barney's left, taking advantage of the distraction, another group of townsfolk also ran towards the steep slope, trying to reach the 'safety' of the trees that stood above it. On both sides of Shine and Barney, the Duke's soldiers engaged the grim determination of ordinary townsfolk. Screams of agony were indistinguishable from screams of victory. Barney and Shine ran as fast as they could through the corridor between the two groups. Although they were spotted, the sentries focussed their attention on those trying to leave. It appeared that Barney was correct – the sentries were more concerned about preventing anyone from leaving the town than entering it.

Barney put his head down and sprinted. Shine, her arms pumping at her sides, had, by this time, caught up with him. She urged him on as she took the lead. They ran straight through the now-vacated outpost where they had seen the sentries take their evening meal. Barney could see the remains of a rabbit's carcass still sitting on a spit above the cooling coals.

Some distance to their right, a group of encircled townsfolk stood back-to-back, thrusting weapons at the sentries who had stopped their flight to freedom.

Barney and Shine were well past the campfire and nearing the first of the town's buildings when the last of the resisting townsfolk were cut down.

Shine reached the beginning of a street between two buildings in front of her.

Barney heard a shout and two paces later an arrow slammed into his backpack, forcefully enough that its tip penetrated the bag, breaking the skin on his back. The impact caused him to stagger and fall. Another two arrows flew through the space where he had been.

With speed borne of desperation, Barney sprang to his feet and ran as fast as he could towards the darkened street. As he reached the corner of the first building, Shine's hand shot out, grasped a flailing arm, and pulled him towards the ruins.

With moments to spare he was removed from the path of several more arrows that had been aimed to strike him down. The arrows flew into darkness, skittering to a stop along the road before several more struck the walls of the building.

"Thanks. Stay. Away. From. Windows," puffed Barney.

Barney and Shine passed through what would have been the main living area and out into a smaller back room that contained discarded remnants of bedding. The rear wall of the building had been shattered by a large boulder.

Pausing for breath, Barney leant against the ruins. His hands were shaking so much that he crossed his arms to try to calm himself down.

Shine grasped his arm fiercely, "We can't stop here."

"They won't follow. They'd have to leave their posts to do that. Just give me a minute," gasped Barney. Shine reached around and pulled the arrow from his pack.

As Barney felt his breathing slow, he nodded to Shine, "Let's go."

The street to the rear of the building was empty. The only sounds that they could hear were the stones of the catapults slamming into the Baron's castle. The barrage had a rhythm to it that sounded strangely like the heartbeat of the legendary giants who, the stories claimed, had once ruled the land.

Barney had been to this area of the town a few times on errands or with friends. He didn't try to follow the main thoroughfares as they were not the most direct route. Moving swiftly, he led Shine into a network of side alleys that twisted and turned around the backs of houses and shops.

Before too long, they came to what had been the main cloth market. The place through which Barney usually had to use his elbows to push people aside was now empty and dark. All that remained to remind them of the purpose of the large square were two abandoned carts resting beneath a ripped awning which, in better times, had protected its stallholders and their wares from the weather.

Turning to Shine he nodded at her. "This is it. Your turn now."

Shine ran to the middle of the square and turned on the spot. Smiling, she pointed to the road that led towards the castle and headed off.

They had walked through two intersections when they heard the tramping of boots behind them.

Barney didn't hesitate. He pulled Shine with him into a narrow alley. The confines of the alley made the shadows deeper; however, it also funnelled echoes further. When Shine stumbled over some unseen rubbish, the resulting noise carried far.

The tramping boots stopped. They changed direction.

Barney and Shine broke into a run. Over the stone paving, twisting and turning around the blind corners of the alleys and then out into wider thoroughfares they sped, before re-entering the network of alleys and lanes. Behind them, they could hear cursing, threats and shouts. "Curfew breakers!" The threats that followed motivated them to keep moving. Barney had the advantage as he knew this part of the town well. He would not surrender that advantage easily. He could hear no dogs and he knew where they would find safety.

The sounds of pursuit diminished as they tore on. The number of following footfalls rapidly decreased. They were ahead, but they could hear that a small number of pursuers closed the gap every time they moved into a wider laneway. In the twisting alleys, they had the advantage. They were nimble, lighter and motivated. In the straighter and broader laneways, the pursuers closed the gap.

Halfway down a narrow alley Barney came to a barred window. The bars crossed each other in a square grid pattern. Stopping Shine, he leapt at the bars after motioning for her to drop her staff. Barney had done this before. He knew that upon climbing to the top of this window, they could spring to a narrow ledge on the other side of the alley and then they simply had to haul themselves up onto the roof. There they could hide. He had seen a pickpocket doing exactly what he was doing now.

Unfortunately, the chase had made him forget his shoulder. Although he had been following Tom's advice and had been working on strengthening it, as soon as he sprang up onto the bars he knew he had a problem. His shoulder was still not strong enough to bear the load.

He collapsed to the ground. There was no way he would be able to pull himself up with the necessary speed. Shine, halfway up, looked down.

"Keep going. Jump from the window to the ledge on the opposite side. Haul yourself up onto the roof and then lie flat in the cavity," he said.

Shine hesitated but he glared at her and she did as she was told. As she disappeared, Barney got up and ran. He had no other option; however, he had lost precious time.

"Stop! Don't move."

A guard had entered the alley. He was alone. He had always been the fastest man in his unit and was proud of the title. He had left the other members of his six-man patrol behind. Only he had been able to keep pace through the chase. Barney backed away.

The guard charged at him. Barney waited.

At the last possible moment, Barney ducked, sidestepped to the left and lashed out with his right leg.

The guard was leaning forward and off balance when Barney's leg connected with his shin, causing him to trip and fall to the ground.

Barney started to run again. However, the guard reacted quickly. He threw his helmet at Barney with such force that when it caught him on his back, it knocked him from his feet. He landed on his back. His attacker rose to his feet. Barney tried to scrabble backwards, crab-like, away from his attacker.

The guard drew his knife and advanced on Barney.

"I said stop!"

Barney faltered to a stop, his hands palm down behind him and his bottom on the ground. He looked up at the man imploringly.

"And now you die."

The guard grasped Barney's hair and raised his knife above his head so that he could sweep it down into Barney's exposed neck.

For the third time in his short life, Barney believed, without a shadow of doubt, that he was going to die. Still, he desperately fumbled for Tom's knife.

Movement from above. Unseen by either of the combatants, Shine fell from the roof with a loose tile in her hands.

The knife swung. Shine fell feet first with the tile gripped tightly in both hands above her head. As Shine closed the distance, she swung the tile down before her, but she missed the man's head. Her weight coupled with her downward momentum combined in an explosive mix as the full force behind the tile struck the man's shoulder, moments before the knife would have ended Barney's life. The force of the blow from the tile was not enough to cut through the man's chainmail, but it was sufficient to crush the man's shoulder. The tile shattered into a thousand pieces, but the force of the blow tore the man's shoulder muscles and broke several bones. His knife spun to a rest at Barney's feet.

As Shine fell to the ground, the impact of the tile pulled the man towards her. Despite his agony, the man clamped his left hand across Shine's throat. His pain fired his adrenaline. He held her airway closed. Shine clawed at him in desperation as her vision blurred, then began to go dark.

Barney thrust the guard's knife into the soft tissue of his exposed neck. The man tried to scream but he was unable to do so. He released Shine and frantically scrambled to pull the knife out and away from the terrible wound. Shine was still gasping for breath when the dead guard fell to the ground at her side.

Looking up, she saw Barney staring down at her. His face was an ashen white. His eyes were wide with shock and despair, but even so, his mind grasped the peril of the situation that they were in.

"We have to go. Quickly. Before anyone else gets here."

Taking his hand, Shine unsteadily got to her feet and retrieved her staff. The two of them melted into the darkness.

CHAPTER

TWELVE

—— ◆ ——

Dawn found Shine and Barney huddled together in a gutter beneath a footbridge. They had spent what little had remained of the night sleeping fitfully. With their teeth chattering from the cold, they had listened to sentries pounding over the bridge as they looked for those who had slain their comrade.

Shortly after the sun rose in the sky, a horn sounded three times. At first, there was no sign of any activity. Barney and Shine wondered at the reason for the signal, but soon enough they heard the movement of shuffling groups of people being led across the bridge.

Landsend had been under strict curfew since the arrival of Duke Jacoby's troops and no one was allowed out during the hours of darkness. The townsfolk, many of whom were relatives of the castle's defenders, were used as human shields that preyed upon the minds and action of Baron Aethelson's troops.

That there were so many townspeople within Landsend was testament to the speed and surprise of the Duke's initial attack. Less than half of the townspeople had been able to escape into either the forest or the castle. Their lives were now controlled by the Duke's army and the sentry system ensured that they stayed within the town.

From what little they could see from their concealed vantage point, Barney and Shine were able to discern that small groups of captive townsfolk were being escorted to collect food and water. The captives were monitored and escorted at all times. They were never left to their own devices.

The escorts would regularly stop on the footbridge to bellow orders and the occasional insult at the prisoners. The guards' proximity caused Barney and Shine to remain still and hidden. They decided that as soon as the sun set, they would try to find André. All they had to do was not be seen.

The hours slid by with the pace of a snail. They lay close together to try to retain warmth. In the late afternoon, as they snacked on their food reserves, Barney, despite himself, began to believe that their goal of remaining undetected was going to be successful.

It was growing cooler when water from a drizzle of rain began to seep into the drain and into their clothes. Suddenly Shine drew her knees into her body with a look of horror on her face.

"There's something in here," she whispered.

The water trickling down through the drain had begun to reduce the dry area around them.

Barney sensed movement at his feet. There was something in the drain with them! A paw rested on his leg. He kicked out. From the resultant squeal he knew exactly what it was. "Rats," he proclaimed quietly with distaste.

The rats were looking for dry land. And as far as they were concerned, that was exactly what Barney and Shine were – dry land.

Shine stifled a scream as a large rat clambered on her chest. Swiftly seizing it, Barney threw it away from them. It landed just short of the edge of the bridge.

"What was that?" they heard someone say above them.

The rat scampered out from under the bridge. A spear missed it by inches. The rat scurried off at top speed.

"You there! Girl! Fetch my spear. Now!"

A young blonde girl, of about five years of age, dropped down from above and gingerly picked her way along the slippery drain to where the spear lay. As she picked it up, she turned back towards the bridge and caught sight of Barney and Shine. She stopped and looked at them.

Barney put his finger on his lips and implored her with his eyes to keep their secret.

The little girl had seen many things over the last few months. Her father, a baker, had been killed before her eyes when he had tried to bar the door against the invaders. Her mother was lying sick in the large house where 'everyone' was kept. She was scared most of the time because the bad men beat anyone they thought was doing the wrong thing. She tried awfully hard not to do the wrong thing and she was very, very tired.

That morning the bad men had been angry because someone had killed one of their friends and they had beaten the old man who had made her shoes for her fourth birthday. Those shoes didn't fit her now and she desperately wanted him to make her new ones.

The boy and the girl under the bridge looked dirty to her. They didn't look mean, but they shouldn't have been there. No one should have been there. Why would anyone choose to lie in a drain unless they were being naughty?

She didn't mean to do it. She just didn't want to be hurt for not doing the right thing.

The little girl lifted her arm and pointed at Barney and Shine.

The man who had thrown the spear was bored. All he wanted to do was to attack the castle; however, he had strict orders to stay away from it, monitor anyone who was in the town and take to the Magistrar any new young male that they discovered – preferably alive.

The soldier saw the little girl point and so did his companion.

In the cramped space below, Barney and Shine tried to react quickly; however, there had been very little room to move in the drain and their muscles were cold and stiff from lying still for so long.

The guards dropped to different sides of the bridge with their swords drawn.

"So, what do we have here then?"

One of the men beckoned for Barney and Shine to come out.

When they weren't quick enough, Barney felt his left foot being seized in a strong grip. Barney was yanked out from under the bridge and away from his backpack. Shine was soon deposited beside him, a sword resting on each of their chests.

"Blood on their clothes. These might be the ones."

"Which group did you escape from?"

Barney looked at the soldier with a puzzled expression. He had no idea how to respond.

"We need him alive, but not her."

"They're only kids. Can't see either of them getting the better of one of us and if they are the killers, then the Magistrar will want to publicly punish them both. Tie 'em up, take his knife and bring 'em to the Magistrar."

Barney was relieved of Tom's knife. Ropes were used to tie his hands together and then his bindings were linked to Shine's.

Looking around them Barney and Shine could see roughly fifteen townspeople, mostly young women and old men, standing in a group, holding pots of water and food. In addition to the two soldiers who had captured them, there were another two standing to one side of the captives. On many of the rooftops, archers looked down on the streets. All the troopers and archers were alert and none of them had any pity in their eyes.

"Can you handle two kids on your own?" asked one of the troopers of the man who had thrown the now-retrieved spear.

The man gave an ugly laugh and motioned with his spear for Barney and Shine to move away from the group.

The little girl stood waving as they were led away, not really knowing whether she had done the right thing.

Shortly after they moved off, the rainfall became heavier.

As Barney and Shine were herded along the town's thoroughfares, they passed several groups of haggard people being led about for unknown reasons. Before too long, they found themselves back in the cloth market and, from there, they were led towards the castle.

The main thoroughfare was wide enough for two carts to pass each other while pedestrians had room to walk on either side. The street was broad and open and devoid of any cover, so they could not avoid becoming soaking wet.

The guard leading Barney and Shine had been stationed in this part of Landsend since the beginning of the occupation. He knew that this street teemed with water during storms. He had been on several patrols looking for townspeople who had not been captured, or simply to keep the peace, so he was familiar with the side streets and some of the alleyways. Not wanting to be in the rain for any longer than necessary he decided to take a covered detour on his way to the Magistrar.

Their escort led them into a narrower laneway that he knew ran towards his intended destination. Immediately they stepped between the buildings, the force of the rain lessened. It was caught by the roofs of the buildings which, some two storeys up, encroached over the laneway. For a time, they would be sheltered from the heaviest of rain and from the eyes of the archers who stood atop many of the roofs.

The guard kicked at Barney to make him move faster.

Barney's yelp caused Shine to look up. As she did, she was startled to recognise a green door at the top of three stone steps that was painted with a sign advertising dyed cloth for sale. It matched the description that André had given her so very long ago. She slowed her pace. The soldier angrily cuffed her on the back of the head, propelling her to catch up with Barney. "Move it." Her eyes remained fixed on the door, imploring it to open so that she might see André.

They continued to move down the laneway, passing sets of stairs that led up to doors of houses and shops and stairways that led down to basements. At one such stairway, Barney detected furtive movement from the corner of his eye. He realised that it was highly unlikely that a member of the Duke's forces would be in hiding. They did not have to skulk in the shadows. Resolutely, Barney didn't flinch or turn his head. He simply hoped.

When the guard passed by the stairway, two figures moved. One leapt for the soldier's legs and the other for his upper body. In a clatter, the three men fell together. The soldier kept hold of his spear, but he had no room to bring it to bear in the confined space. A hand was roughly clamped over the guard's mouth to prevent him from calling out as his head was pushed backwards, with force, against the cobbled surface of the laneway. The soldier passed into unconsciousness before he could raise the alarm.

Barney, with his hands still tied, was unsure whether to run. However, as one of the two figures turned to look up at them Shine knew exactly who he was. "André!" she exclaimed with delight. She virtually pulled Barney off his feet in her rush to get to her beau.

André was a tall, mature-looking youth with an olive complexion and slicked-back hair. Barney estimated that André was older than he was. He was thickset, muscular and obviously fit.

"Shine, what are you doing here?"

Disregarding the fact that Barney and Shine were tied together, André picked himself up and rushed over to Shine, taking her in an embrace that explained to Barney why Shine was desperate to move away from the farm and into the township. André looked intently at Barney over Shine's shoulder. He nodded his head at Barney as he assessed him.

After cutting the ropes that bound her, André held Shine tightly for a long moment.

Eventually, Barney said irritably, "Guys, I'm sorry, but we must go. Now. Before the alarm is raised."

A flushed Shine turned to Barney, "This is André. We have known each other for a while. Thank you for helping me find him."

"Why would you bring her here – into danger?"

Shine saved Barney from having to respond. "Because I gave him no choice." Her tone stopped any further argument.

As much as André knew that it would have been highly unlikely that Shine's companion would have been unable to resist her stubbornness, he resented the fact that Shine had, unnecessarily, been placed in danger. He was also unhappy with the way in which Barney looked at Shine, however, at that moment there was very little he could do about the source of his unhappiness, so he went over to where the guard lay prone on the ground. He relieved the guard of his sword and strapped it to his waist. His companion recovered the spear, a knife and a purse of coins. Taking Shine's hand, André led them away from the scene. Barney bowed his head and shuffled behind.

André led Barney and Shine towards Old Town. As they cautiously navigated the streets and alleys André explained to them that he and his associate had been out scavenging for supplies when they had come across Barney and Shine, whom they hadn't recognised. Knowing that they could not be seen by the archers who patrolled the rooftops, they had attacked the guard with the hope of freeing their 'fellow citizens' and recovering some weapons.

André took them to the cellar of a house where they were introduced to a number of dirty and dishevelled individuals, mostly male, who were hiding from the Duke's forces.

André explained that their group contained some of the many townsfolk who had not been captured. Each night, due to food shortages, some of the captive townsfolk tried to escape the town, however, as Shine and Barney had already witnessed, escape was rarely successful. Most of the 'free' townspeople who remained had decided to wait out the Duke's occupation by hiding in what remained of their town. The occupiers were taking every precaution against people leaving and any captured males were taken before the Magistrar, who questioned them at length before they simply disappeared.

Their group was by no means an organised resistance; they were merely intent on finding a way to survive until the Duke's men were defeated or withdrew. They rarely attacked any of the occupying force except on an opportunistic basis when the odds were heavily stacked in their favour. Times were tough. They had looted most of the known sources of food and water. Resources of any kind were now in short supply.

They were introduced and stories were exchanged. When the novelty of their presence had worn off Barney sought out André and Shine, "I'm going to find my mother tonight."

"From the moment that you leave this cellar you will be putting your life at risk. As I have already told you – the soldiers are actively seeking out male youth. They will take you to the Magistrar –" André began.

"I wasn't asking your permission. I was telling you what I am going to do."

"You're a fool. Going closer to the castle will place you at risk of being targeted by both the Duke's forces and the Baron's forces. You will not find your mother."

"I've come this far, and I have no intention of starving to death in this cellar. I will deliver my news to my mother."

André went to rise but Shine placed pressure on his arm, "Barney has every right to find out for himself whether his mother is alive, and I have promised him that I would assist him, just as he assisted me to find you."

"You're both crazy. It was sheer luck that you found me."

"Be that it as it may, I will be going with him and... and I need you to come with us."

André frowned and rubbed his forehead with the palms of his hands. He felt the urge to throw Barney out onto the street and leave him to his own devices, but he knew, in his heart, that if he took that course of action, he would risk losing Shine. He was torn between the need to protect her and the need to please her.

"Please," whispered Shine in his ear.

André fingered the hilt of his newly acquired sword. At the very least he could protect her – although he wouldn't dare say that to her. He could feel the pressure of Shine's hand on his arm. If Barney's mother was alive, then perhaps they could leave him with her. He felt his resistance to the idea begin to break down.

"You don't understand the risks involved. That part of town is subject to artillery barrages from both sides. The Duke's soldiers have already gone through every building. No one is living there –"

"Could you live with yourself if I had been living there and you didn't take up the opportunity to see if I had survived?" asked Shine quietly.

"That's not the point. I do not want you to risk your life on a senseless mission."

Shine's tone took on a harder edge, "Since when has taking a risk for family been senseless?"

"Perhaps I could take him while you stay here. The smaller the party, the better the odds."

Shine raised her left eyebrow but said nothing in response.

André knew the look well. Shine used it, perhaps subconsciously or perhaps intentionally, to signify that she had made up her mind and so for her the argument was over. He had two choices: commit to the idea or commit to a fruitless argument that would end with her storming from his presence and doing what he objected to anyway.

André still felt conflicted. He couldn't help thinking that Barney didn't look like he'd be useful in a fight. To survive, Shine needed every bit of help that he could offer to her, and she had admitted that she needed him.

Inwardly, André groaned. He knew that his feelings tied him to Shine and when he turned and looked at Shine, he found that her eyes were boring into his.

"Fine. I'll come," he mumbled.

Shine rewarded him with a kiss on the cheek. His conflicted emotions had been obvious to her, and she regretted having to push the issue. She looked to Barney, "Get some sleep. Come and get us when you are ready."

Barney, Shine and André rested in the cellar while they waited for the afternoon sun to wane. As twilight settled over the town, Barney had them tie cloth over the soles of their shoes to deaden the noise of their footfalls. Then he took soot from the fire pit and rubbed it into his face to blacken and disguise his features. André saw the sense in what he was doing and followed Barney's lead, but it took some time before Shine could be persuaded to join in.

An hour after the sun had set and well after the horns were sounded to signal the start of the curfew, they slunk out of the cellar and into the laneway.

Barney led the way. Unlike the night before, he stuck to the shadows wherever possible and avoided any of the main thoroughfares. At the slightest sound, he stopped dead and signalled for the others to do likewise.

The journey from the cellar to his home would usually have taken no more than three-quarters of an hour to walk on the busiest of days. Now it took far longer. Time and time again they were forced to stop or divert from their path to avoid patrols or the routes that were being watched by the sentries whose silhouettes they could make out on the rooftops against the night sky. Their cautious approach took time but enabled them to stay out of sight.

The closer that they got to Barney's home, the more imposing the castle looked and the more destruction that was evident. Blackened and burnt homes and shops became more apparent, as did the wayward boulders which, after being hurled from catapults, had dropped short or simply been off target. Barney felt sad as he saw the destruction that had been visited upon many of his favourite childhood haunts.

The ruins helped rather than hindered them. The blocks of stone and the heaps of thatch, tiles and wooden beams cast their own shadows, creating cover from the eyes of the sentries.

The nearer that they came to the castle, the more noise they could hear emanating from it as the Baron's men worked to repair its defences. They also felt, not just heard, the impact of the boulders on the castle walls as the ceaseless bombardment continued.

Following Barney's directions, they wound their way through Old Town until they finally came to a row of three homes, only one of which remained undamaged. By this time, they were on their bellies, sliding and crawling between objects to keep concealed from the view of the Duke's patrols and the Baron's sentries.

Barney stopped in front of the undamaged cottage. It was closest of the cottages to the castle's imposing six-storey walls and so it was well within range of the flight of an arrow that, at any time, might be fired down at them.

Motioning for the others to stay, Barney warily worked his way on his stomach over the ground to the door and pushed it open. The hinges groaned; a surprisingly loud noise given the sounds that were coming from all around them.

He paused, waiting for any sound of movement from within the cottage.

Hearing nothing untoward, he rose to a crouch and pushed his way inside.

His home was a small guardsman's cottage. Immediately at the entrance of the cottage, which had been in his family for several generations, was the main room. It contained a large communal table where many a meal had been eaten and many a lively lecture from his mother had been delivered. To his right, there was a kitchen with a metal stove which still had a rack that Barney had worked hard to keep full of wood. The rack extended from the floor to the ceiling. When he was younger he had needed to climb on a chair to reach the top of it. Directly in front of him, beyond the dining area, was a curtained area in which his parents had slept and, to his left, a far smaller curtained area that was his bedroom. The flooring was largely wooden except for part of the kitchen which was paved in stone so that any wood that escaped the fire did not set the building alight.

The main table now lay overturned, and the chairs were strewn across the floor. His father's chess set was scattered all over the floor. Clearly, there had been some form of scuffle. The partition to his parents' area had been torn down and thrown to one side and the curtain to the area where he had slept lay open.

Moving quickly, he passed through to where his parents had once slept. Empty. From behind him, he heard movement at the door. As he turned, Shine and André slipped into his home.

There was nothing to indicate that Barney's mother had recently been home. From the dust and cold hearth, it was obvious that no one had stayed in the cottage for some time.

Barney went to his bed and without pause, he knelt and felt under it. There it was, his pride and joy; the bow that his father had bought for him. From the moment it was in his hands, Barney had realised that the power of the bow was not something that was a matter for luck. He planned to learn to predict the flight of the arrow. It was not a weapon of strength but of skill and finesse; a skill that would take a long time for him to come anywhere near to mastering. But Barney had chosen to accept the challenge. He was above average but by no means a crack shot and his training had so far revolved around stationary targets and repetitive accuracy, but this bow and its quiver of arrows were among the few things that truly belonged to him. He believed that he had the same chance as anyone else of becoming a skilled bowman. His father had hoped that his ability to read would enable him to become a scribe, but Barney had realised that although reading may have led him to quicker promotions through the ranks, most scribes came from upper or merchant class families or the monasteries.

The bow was a three-quarter size longbow used when young people began their training. Its draw-weight was less than a full-size bow so its range was less; however, it had been tailored to take into account the developing strength of the youth who would use it. Eventually, he would progress to a full-size bow when both his accuracy and strength had improved.

The bow was his and it was coming with him.

Barney then saw the long stout staff that his father had used on his night patrols to enforce the Baron's law in the town. Taking the staff, he gave it to Shine. It would be of no use to him; however, he knew that Shine could wield a staff.

Barney was at a loss as to what to do now that he had made it home and found it empty.

From the kitchen, he heard Shine hesitantly speak, "Barney, come here."

"What?"

"Look," she said, pointing to the floor between the fireplace and the kitchen cupboards.

Barney looked down, puzzled for a moment. Then realisation dawned upon him. The timber and stone of the floor were stained almost black from something spilt on it. He searched his memory for anything that might have been there before he had left on that fateful day with his father's last patrol. Nothing came to mind. The stain was from an event that had occurred after he had gone away. Something or someone had been dragged towards the doorway of the cottage.

Barney crouched to the floor, caressing his hand over the area. He knew what Shine was getting at. She believed that this dark stain resulted from a vast amount of blood that had been spilt upon the floor. Could this be where my mother died? He had no way of knowing. He was filled with disbelief and grief. He stilled his hand upon the floor, hoping that the wood itself would share its knowledge with him.

Shine put a hand on his shoulder. "We can't stay here, Barney. We have to leave Landsend while we still can."

"Where's the closest group of prisoners?" Barney responded, with the fierce determination of someone suffering from the realisation and guilt of being the only surviving member of an entire family.

André responded quickly, "Barney – we can't. There is no way that we can help those people. There are only three of us."

Barney glared at him. "Follow me, or don't follow me, I don't care. I need information and I'm going to get it with or without you."

Both Shine and André were taken aback by the fierce sense of purpose that radiated from Barney. For a moment neither of them reacted. They stared at each other for a time. Then, Shine sighed and said, "You might as well tell him André, or he'll just go blundering about looking anyway."

With shoulders slumped in defeat, André confirmed that the closest of the captive camps was between them and the rear of the castle, northwest of their position.

Barney went to the table beside his parents' bed and placed his father's signet ring upon it. He paused a moment as he rested it in place. Barney then moved back through the door, touching the doorframe as he left in a silent gesture of goodbye and thanks. Shine and André followed close behind him.

FOURTEEN

———✦———

Barney's family home was in Old Town, about three-quarters of the way down the western wall of the castle. Each of the walls of the castle had an archers' tower in the middle and at either end. These rectangular towers jutted out from the walls to give the defenders an unhindered view of the base of the walls. The towers were connected by battlements that were patrolled by sentries at random intervals.

The Duke's main attack was focussed on the front gate of the castle at the southern side of the castle. The strongest of the castle's defences were on the northern wall as that was, historically, the direction from which all the enemies of the Kingdom had come. When the Duke's initial surprise attack to secure the gates had failed, he had sent his artillery to breach the southern entrance by pounding it with rocks and other projectiles.

The majority of the Duke's forces were gathered where they believed the walls would be breached by the bombardment. His remaining forces occupied the town to ensure that the besieged castle was cut off from supplies and reinforcements.

The entrance of the castle was a three-stage gate consisting of a drawbridge that was lowered down over a deep manmade trench, which was well supplied with water from the castle's spring. The second stage of the defences consisted of a large iron portcullis which opened into a marshalling area. A large set of oak doors, inlaid with iron, was the final stage of the entrance. On each side of the marshalling area, there was a tall stone wall from the top of which archers could fire if an invading force breached both the drawbridge and the portcullis.

The area between the last of the buildings of the surrounding town and the castle had been kept clear of any large permanent structures but, over time, when no large northern force had attacked, complacency had set in and some utility buildings, such as stables and cattle yards, had been constructed in that area. A large number of captives were held in these stalls and stables. They were locked in at night and paraded during the day. The defenders of the castle risked killing their own people if they showered the area with projectiles.

The group of captives that André led them to were housed in an old stable. The stable's yards were empty, but the main building was crammed with townspeople. Guards patrolled the perimeter to ensure that no one escaped. The three of them approached the stable silently and slowly. They kept an eye on the guards and took advantage of the shadows and structures that broke the sentries' line of sight.

What neither Barney nor his companions could see was the activity, high above them, on the castle walls. A group of troopers had gathered under the cover of darkness and had worked to secure three ropes to the innermost side of the battlement.

In the marshalling area, a large group of the Baron's cavalry had gathered silently before the portcullis which was slowly being raised by a series of chains that ran through a recently greased windlass mechanism. For the moment, the presence of the cavalry was concealed by the raised drawbridge. Above the cavalry, the winches, windlass and counterweights that enabled the chains to draw up both the portcullis and the drawbridge were manned by dozens of the Baron's strongest men. The horses sensed the tension. Some pawed at the stone floor. They had been bred for war and now, despite their lack of recent exercise, they were anxious to carry their charges into battle. The Baron busied himself by giving final instructions to the officer who was stationed at the very front of the cavalry line.

***

In the faint light, Barney counted the guards. At least six were actively patrolling the stable and a further eight or so were, due to the late hour, off-watch and sleeping at various campfires.

Barney, Shine and André crept closer.

***

The Baron shook the hand of the Commander of his Household Cavalry and then signalled to a man watching him from the tower above.

When the Baron's signal was relayed to the men on the ramparts, they lowered three thick ropes over the side.

Collectively, the Baron's men held their breath, but they needn't have worried; the ropes were hidden from view in the shadows cast by the towers and the sentries about the stable were more interested in preventing their captives from escaping than an improbable break out from the castle. The ropes snaked downwards until they came to rest with their tips resting lightly on the ground.

***

Barney found a place where the patrolling guard passed, for a short time, out of sight of a door to the stable.

"Take my bow, give me a knife and stay here," he said to André.

Stealthily, he slid along the ground toward the building.

***

The first three men, using every endeavour to stay in the shadows, lowered themselves down the ropes towards the ground.

***

When the patrolling guard moved out of sight, Barney sprang to his feet and sprinted to the stable door, counting as he did so to enable him to judge when the sentry would return. Drawing back the latch, he stepped inside and closed the door behind him.

***

Reaching the ground, the three troopers took position near the ropes, crouching low to the ground with swords drawn, as they beckoned the next three to follow.

***

Barney rapidly cast his eye over the sleeping forms in the stable but none of them was his mother. It appeared that despite his best hopes, she was not here. No one stirred. Finally, he saw a sleeping form that he did recognise – the old man who had sold him vegetables from his garden. He approached him slowly.

Barney placed his hand over the old man's mouth and shook him awake. Startled, the man opened his eyes and attempted to draw away.

"Be still and quiet, old man. I mean you no harm," whispered Barney.

Surprised recognition dawned on the man's face, and he nodded his response. Barney slowly removed his hand.

"My mother. Where is she?" whispered Barney.

The old man shook his head, "I'm sorry son, but she is gone from this world. When they cleared the buildings closest to the castle, she resisted. We tried to get them to take her to the healers, but it was too late. You need to go, or they will take you."

Barney felt tears prick into the corners of his eyes. For a moment he felt guilty, lost and utterly alone.

***

The next three men reached the ground, drew their swords and, before prostrating themselves on the ground, beckoned the remaining seven to follow. The youngest of the party, linked via a safety rope to one of the more experienced troopers, gingerly lowered himself over the side and began to inch his way down.

As the youth reached the ground, a member of the vanguard cut through the safety rope. The twelve soldiers formed a protective circle around the youth. As one, they began to move. Unfortunately, they startled a rat that had been foraging for food. The rat, suspecting an imminent attack from a predator, made haste to scamper away.

If it hadn't been for the rat's rapid movement, the Baron's men might have been able to exploit their disguise as members of the Duke's army and escaped into the night. However, the periphery vision of one of the stable guards caught the movement. When he turned and focussed, he immediately made out the figures at the foot of the wall and the ropes dangling to the ground behind them.

"Alarm! By the wall."

Far above them, one of the Baron's men sounded his horn. The drawbridge creaked downwards, the clanking chain an obvious signal of the Baron's intentions. As he had been instructed to do, the youth sprang to the middle rope, wound it around his waist and grasped it tightly with both hands. The rope was immediately drawn upwards.

Three arrows pierced the air above the boy's head. In a panic, the boy let go of the rope. He fell back to the ground, landing behind the protective row of men.

Inside the stable Barney bit down on his lip, using the pain to force away his urge to collapse in tears. Because of him Shine was in danger. It was time for him to face his future and help his friend. As the horn sounded from above, Barney moved quickly to the door.

The horn had set off more shouting, waking the people in the stable. Barney partially opened the door so he could peer out. The guards to the rear of the building appeared to have left their posts at the sound of the alarm. When Barney cautiously pushed the door open and stepped outside, he saw that the guards had all gathered at the front of the stable. Some of them were now shooting arrows at a small group who were standing near the castle wall.

From the castle's walls, archers fired back.

Another horn sounded; this time from one of the Duke's men.

To the front of the castle, cavalry streamed out over the lowered drawbridge, intent on circling around to where the Baron's men were shielding the youth.

From deep inside Barney, rage and a sense of helplessness welled and threatened to engulf him. Events, over which he had no control or influence, had shattered his life. He was adrift in events that were beyond his understanding, and he ached to regain some semblance of control.

André was signalling him, with bow in hand, to hurry. In a moment of clarity, Barney knew what he wanted to do.

Without being conscious of moving, Barney found himself standing in front of André, watching his lips move. But Barney heard no sound. He snatched his bow and quiver from André's grasp and dropped André's knife at his feet. With bow in hand, he turned and, as he moved forward, he notched an arrow. He ran along the side of the stable.

Once he was at the front of the stable he could see where the Duke's guards had stationed themselves. Barney kept moving until he had a clear line of sight. He stopped and planted his feet, drew back on the bowstring, took aim along the arrow's shaft, visualised the shot and fired. The arrow took flight, speeding across the narrow distance and struck the archer closest to him. The archer fell forward, clutching his shoulder. As the archer fell, the sound of the commotion around him came roaring back to Barney.

The other archers were unaware of the danger. They assumed that their comrade had been felled by an arrow from the ramparts. Once more, Barney fired and another archer fell. This time, some of the remaining guards realised that they were in danger from behind. Turning, three of them drew their swords and ran towards Barney.

André shouldered Barney aside and met the first sword with his own. Shine swung her staff at the man's legs, shattering a knee.

André parried a blow from the second man and Shine stood at his side, swinging her staff at the third. Barney trusted in André and Shine's abilities and ignored the skirmish, sending another shot at the archers.

From inside the stable, there was a roar of defiance. Then, as one, the occupants of the building burst out and fled from the building in separate directions, some towards safety and others to help André and Shine. The old man lost his life when he ran between a sword and Shine's back, but that distraction saved her life. It gave her time to swing the staff above her head and bring it down with enough force to knock her attacker from his feet.

As the last of the three men fell to André's sword, Barney felled another archer just as he loosed a shot at the men at the foot of the castle's wall.

Many of the youth's companions lay dead or dying about him. Gaps had appeared where before there had been none. The flight of the final arrow passed between the youth's defenders, striking the boy in his back as he made an attempt to climb one of the ropes back up the wall. The boy's body convulsed in agonising pain that quickly overloaded his senses. The rope slipped from his grasp. Darkness enveloped his vision. His body, in self-preservation mode, cut off his senses to stop the pain. He collapsed to the ground, unconscious.

The Commander of the Baron's Household Cavalry led his men directly towards the skirmish. The iron-shod hooves of the horses pounded the ground into submission.

The Duke's men were streaming from the town and rapidly converging on the scene.

A rider reached the group. The youth's body was thrust at him. He grabbed the prone form and swung it up in front of him. As he spurred his mount, his horse was shot from under him. The Duke's men were coming from all directions now.

From above, the castle's defenders attempted to pick off the Duke's troops – a perilous job considering that the melee was disjointed and free-flowing.

The stampede of people from the stable saved many of the Baron's troops that night. The Duke's reinforcements were initially uncertain about whether they were armed soldiers and so they stopped to chase and engage them, which in turn delayed their arrival at the site of the skirmish. Time and time again, they found themselves chasing down townsfolk before turning their attention back to the castle's defenders.

The Commander reached down and grasped the youth's tunic before slinging the boy over the pommel of his saddle. He sawed on his reins in a desperate attempt to turn his mount back towards the castle's gates and safety.

As the horse turned, the Commander was hit by three arrows. He lurched backwards. As he did, he hauled on his reins. The confused horse turned and charged directly towards the stable.

Barney saw them coming. André was standing to his left and Shine to his right. Barney shouldered his bow and with arms out wide, stood before the horse. A part of him wanted the horse to ride over him.

At the last moment the horse reared, thrashing his hooves at Barney. Both his rider and the youth were thrown to the ground. The riderless horse turned and galloped towards the castle gates and his stablemates, confident that he had done the right thing.

"We've got to get out of here, right now!" cried André.

As André turned to lead them away, Barney heard the youth groan.

Suddenly, as if from nowhere, one of the Duke's soldiers appeared and leapt towards the youth, "I've got him!" he yelled.

For some reason, Barney felt calm. These people had taken everything from him. Everything. Now they wanted something, and he would take it from them. He shrugged his bow from his shoulder and loaded it as if he was on the practice range. Pulling back, he fired in one swift and smooth movement that would have earned him high praise from any range-master. The arrow caught the man in his side, below his raised arm. Impeded by the man's armour, the arrow did not reach any significant organs; however, it penetrated far enough to cause the man to collapse to the ground. As he struggled to rise, Shine swung her staff above her head and brought it down with all her strength on his helmet, compressing it against his skull. The man fell back to the ground and didn't move.

Barney reached the youth. Despite appearances, the boy was around thirteen years of age. He was unconscious and had an arrow lodged firmly in his back below his shoulder blade.

Shine was instantly at his side. Together they picked the boy up.

They were at the point of convergence of all the incoming combatants, but, for the moment, the four of them stood alone in the calm eye of a storm. Nearest the wall, the last of the Baron's men had formed a line. The horsemen were milling around, leaderless now that their Commander could not be seen. Foot soldiers were erupting from the castle. From the town, the Duke's men were coming at the run. The freed captives were still running from the stable in ones and twos in random directions and the last of the Duke's men who had been guarding the stable were either engaged with the horsemen or were falling back. The archers on the castle wall had largely ceased firing as they had no way of knowing who was friend or who was foe.

"André! Take the boy!" yelled Barney.

André slung the boy over his shoulder, rather like a sack of potatoes.

The Baron's men had been cooped up in the castle for a long time and they were thirsting for a fight. They saw the Duke's men coming from the town and they charged forward.

Barney pointed in a direction parallel to the castle walls but between the lines of the two converging forces and started to run.

Crouching low, using whatever cover that they could find, they ran. The archers on both sides started firing arrows, but since the companions were not wearing the Baron's or the

Duke's colours, and were clearly not posing a threat to anyone, only a few arrows were aimed their way. The soldiers on either side of them had been denied a fight for too long and now, with the opportunity at hand, they snarled and proceeded to target each other in a vicious attempt to gain the upper hand.

The flanks of the two opposing forces began to close around them, like the jaws of a steel trap coming together. The companions manoeuvred swiftly, navigating through the narrow gaps amid the combatants.

Barney ran headfirst into one of the Duke's men and the impact knocked them both off their feet. One of the Baron's men seized his opportunity and ferociously swung his sword down at the trooper. Barney's presence was forgotten, and he took the opportunity to leave the life-and-death struggle behind him.

Someone lunged at Shine with his sword. As she parried it with her staff, André plunged a knife into the man's ribs, leaving it in place when it became entangled in the soldier's tunic. They ran on.

"Don't stop to engage!" yelled Barney as he swung his bow at the head of a man to distract him from targeting André, "Run!"

Barney sidestepped the arc of the man's sword that would have lethally struck his neck. The man's follow-through caused him to overbalance. Barney struck him behind his knee with his bow, causing him to stumble. This gained Barney valuable seconds and the man a new opponent. Without waiting to see the effect of his action, Barney ran to catch up with Shine and André. He watched as Shine rammed one end of her staff savagely into the ribs of a man who had stepped in front of her. The blow drove the air from his lungs, giving her vital moments to move on.

André, hampered by the boy, ran into space between two combatants, who, glancing at him, paused for an easy kill. Spinning on the spot, André grabbed hold of the boy's breeches and his shirt and used the boy as a human missile. He threw the boy at the trooper on his left. The man's eyes registered shock and grew wide as the boy flew towards him. He made an ungainly attempt to avoid the unusual missile. Continuing his spin, André rotated onto one knee, extended his right hand, in which he now held his sword, and cut through the unprotected calf muscle of his second assailant's left leg.

Despite the boy being small and light, his weight was sufficient to knock André's target off his feet. As André rushed to collect the boy, the man struggled to rise but he was knocked unconscious by Shine, who struck him across his forehead. Shine was panting from her exertions.

Nodding his thanks to Shine, André flipped the boy back over his shoulder and together they all ran on.

They broke free of the fighting without further incident and reached the relative safety of the alleys of Old Town into which they had to move quickly to avoid the sporadic groups of reinforcements who were running down the streets. These troopers were anxious to fight. They could see the Baron's colours before them. Some of them also saw Barney and his companions, but they were largely indifferent to them. The bloodlust of the reinforcements was focussed on the colours of the besieged. They saw no reason to chase a party of youths who clearly had no intention of putting up a fight. Barney led his companions into the maze of twisting alleys and away from the sounds of the fight.

They had run for some time before Barney realised that they needed to rest. Ahead of him, he saw a shop door hanging from its hinges. He barged through the door and flung himself into the room beyond it as the others breathlessly followed.

Outside the companions heard trumpets sounding. Orders were shouted and men committed to battle as more of the castle occupants disgorged themselves from the castle with all the pent-up aggression of the confined. Officers on both sides tried to gain control of their men, but nothing was going to plan. Amidst the chaotic clash, the absence of any ability to enforce a formation or battle plan meant that many lives were needlessly lost.

In the deserted shop, André deposited the boy on a table and paused to stretch his back. Running with a deadweight over one shoulder through an uneven war zone had taken its toll on him.

The arrow that had hit the boy was broken. Probably from when he was thrown. Part of the shaft, and the head of the arrow, remained in the boy's flesh. At a guess, Barney surmised that the arrow tip was lodged firmly in the boy's shoulder blade. He bent to pull the arrow out.

"No," panted Shine, "Leave it there. You could do more damage than good by removing it. Pack the area around the shaft with cloth so it can't move. Then bandage up the entire area. Check my pack for the poultices and bandages that Lucy gave us. Hurry, before he bleeds to death!"

Barney used one of André's knives to cut through the boy's silk shirt. He lathered Lucy's ointments on the wound and then used their entire supply of bandages, and the boy's shirt, to secure the arrow shaft in its position. He managed to slow the bleeding but without proper care, the boy would be in real trouble.

"He'll slow us down. We should leave him here," said André.

Shine and Barney looked at him and shook their heads in unison before Barney said, "No. They want him. We will keep him with us until we find out why."

"Shine, we can't take him," implored André, ignoring Barney's response.

Shine looked at André. Once more, despite her obvious feelings for André, she sided with Barney. She shook her head and responded with steel in her voice, "No. We take him."

André glanced at Barney and then back at Shine. He was clearly annoyed at Shine. He wondered at Barney's influence over Shine's decision-making.

Shine caught André's chain of thoughts. She rose and hugged him tightly before she whispered something in his ear.

"Ok," responded André gruffly, while staring at Barney over her shoulder.

***

The opposing forces were now concentrated around the gates of the castle. The defenders had been forced back across the drawbridge and beyond the portcullis. They were now desperately trying to prevent the Duke's men from breaking through the final door to the castle. Out of necessity the defenders, unlike the attackers, were no longer seeking individual honours. They had begun to work as a united front.

From up high on the castle walls the order came for oil to be thrown down. The contents of large earthen jars cascaded down. The Duke's troops slipped and slid on the ground as the Baron's men heeded their orders to execute a controlled retreat, back through the final internal door.

Desperation pushed the Duke's men forward; many were oblivious to the oil. They were all completely focussed on the men in front of them. They killed or were killed. Most neither smelt nor understood the danger.

As the last of the surviving Baron's men retreated, all that stood between the Duke's forces and victory were the final large oak doors. The Baron signalled. The brake on the chain that held up the huge and heavy metal barrier was released. In an instant, the portcullis sped down, coming to rest within the ranks of the Duke's men. At another signal from the Baron, archers dipped their arrows in pitch and lit them from torches on the battlements.

The archers released their arrows and they shot down into the oil pooled on the ground. The oil burst into flames almost immediately. The Duke's men, who had been pushing towards the castle, were reduced to a mindless rabble. Their only thought was to escape the flames, but they could neither advance nor retreat.

***

Barney could see the glow of the fires from the doorway and could hear the unworldly screams of the dying.

"We must leave now. They won't be able to look for us until morning at the earliest. They have bigger things to worry about at the moment."

Once again, the boy was bundled over André's shoulder, but this time they stepped much more cautiously into the night.

FIFTEEN

— ✦ —

The abandoned house where they chose to spend the rest of the night was not far from where they had entered the town some two nights before. It was in what had once been one of the quieter areas of the town, away from the main thoroughfare but near enough to the markets so that it was not a great burden to carry household supplies to it.

No trumpet sounded that morning to end the curfew. The air was still. The smell of smoke hung heavily in the air, but it was not enough to deter the first of the carrion feeders that circled high above the castle's ramparts.

When Barney was woken for his watch, he rose sleepily to look out of the windows to see if he could make out the placement of the sentries between the last of the buildings and the edge of the valley. What he saw startled him. While he had been asleep, a dramatic change had occurred.

Before the events of the night, the town had been surrounded by a simple ring of campfires, but now there were tents, horses and many soldiers on stretchers and some on makeshift beds. A field hospital had been set up between them and freedom.

The boy groaned. "Water," he pleaded softly through dry lips.

Barney looked around. He had forgotten about the boy. There was no pump in the house and anything of use had been looted from the house a long time ago.

Shaking his head, he moved back to the window. The rush of stubbornness, borne of his grief and his desire to withhold from the Duke's troops something that they wanted, had worn off and he now reasoned that it probably hadn't been his best idea to bring the boy. He sighed as he looked at him again: as his father had often said, making a decision was the easy part – living with the consequences was much harder. He couldn't shift his feeling of responsibility for the lad, and he struggled with the idea of completely abandoning him to his fate.

Barney turned back to the window and watched the scene playing out before him. It was obvious that the number of wounded had been unanticipated and there were frequent arguments over the delays and order of treating the wounded. Barney also noted that despite the fact the night's events had long since passed, wounded were still being carried out from the town and to the aid station.

The boy groaned again.

It was well past midday when André and Shine awoke. By that time the aid station was overflowing, and townspeople were being pressed into service to bring water, food and other supplies.

The boy's groans were much softer now.

"We need a disguise. I'm going to get what we need," announced Barney with the conviction of someone who believed that he had a plan.

"Huh?" André replied.

"We'll drop the boy off at the aid station so that he can be cared for and then we'll use the cover of darkness to be away from there. Besides, we need water."

Shine hissed her disbelief at what she was hearing.

"Agreed!" responded André.

"Look. The boy is in a bad way, and we can't care for him. They won't look for him under their noses. At the aid station, he'll get the care that we can't provide. It will be best for him if we leave him. We just need to get him there, make sure he is safe and then when it's dark, we will make for the trees."

But Shine was far from enthusiastic, "So we use him to our advantage and then, when we don't have any further use for him, we just discard him? We can't just leave him; he's our responsibility."

The argument swayed back and forth, but for once Shine was unable to get her way. Barney's logic coupled with André's agreement was hard to deny and eventually, despite her doubts, Shine reluctantly relented.

Barney wondered at Shine's surrender to his plan. He had steeled himself for a much more fiery response. Then he realised that Shine didn't know the boy and her loyalties rested with himself and André. Shine was doing what she believed, deep down, was best for all three of them, however distasteful that course of action was to her.

When all was decided Barney steeled himself and stepped alone from the house, out into the cobbled streets, leaving Shine and André to tend to their patient as best they could.

Barney immediately felt exposed and almost naked in the light of day. Without the embrace of darkness, he knew that he would eventually be seen by the town's occupiers. He recalled how he had slipped into Marydale by pretending to be with his sister on an errand to collect mushrooms. In that case, the Duke's men had seen what they had wanted to see. Barney knew that they would now be on high alert and suspicious of furtive movements. He decided to put his faith in portraying himself as someone with purpose, someone who was meant to be moving through the streets in the light of day. Squaring his shoulders, he marched to the centre of the road and headed back in the general direction of the castle, striding purposefully and turning his head as if searching for something or someone.

The sentry who was standing on the rooftop of the two-storey inn had not seen where the young man had come from. He could have sworn that the road had been empty just moments before. He gestured at a patrol below him and pointed in the youth's direction. Notching an arrow in his bow, he waited. The young man looked like he was on a mission.

He was making no attempt to hide, not running and he was highly visible; it was only that confidence in movement that stayed the sentry's hand. The patrol drew their swords and took position with their backs to a wall, waiting for the unknown youth to pass by their hiding place.

As Barney strode by the hidden soldiers, they stepped out to meet him. One of them threw a punch. Even though Barney had not been attempting to hide, the swift appearance of the patrol surprised him. The blow connected squarely with the side of his face, knocking him off his feet and onto the street. He was quickly surrounded by a ring of hobnailed boots. He could feel the blood from a cut on his forehead flowing down the side of his face below his already swelling eye.

"Please sirs, I mean no harm," he squealed, as he held out a hand, as if to ward off further blows.

"Identify yourself," said one of the men.

"My name is Preston Mills. I come from Marydale where, until recently, I was apprenticed to the baker. I was told to find the Captain of the Guard to deliver a message," babbled Barney.

The men hesitated. They could kill the lad, take the body to the Magistrar and be done with it, but to do so would be to risk the wrath of the Captain. After the events of the previous night, it would not be wise to be the focus of the Captain's attention.

"What's the message?"

Barney's right eye had already swollen shut and it felt as if the whole of the side of his face was swelling. "Are you the Captain? I was told he had red hair," he said as he squinted through his one good eye.

"Don't mess with me, lad. Give. Me. The. Message!"

Barney didn't have to pretend that he was scared. He was scared. His plan to pass quickly through the town and go about his business had failed miserably. Despite the situation, he was unable to prevent his mind scorning his foolish assumptions. If he hadn't been in such danger, he would have laughed in despair at his own presumptuousness. He now remembered that the Duke's army had been ordered to capture and bring any and all young men before the Magistrar for questioning. Unlike in Marydale, the whole of the Duke's army was on the lookout for someone who looked exactly like him.

Barney quietly berated himself for believing what he wanted to believe. It was just as Bertrand had said: despite everything that he had known, he had been unable to see what was clearly in front of him. He had no one to blame other than himself.

He was well aware that his life was in the balance so, thinking quickly and remembering the list of herbs that Lucy had once asked him to get for her mother from Marydale, he said, "I have details of herbs and supplies that the healers need to treat the wounded. They need more than they have, and they need the Captain to authorise for parties to be sent back to Marydale to collect more."

Again, the men hesitated.

"Well, he don't look like he could carry a sword let alone wield one," said one of the men.

"We is ordered to bring boys from Landsend, not Marydale, to the Magistrar. Let's take him to the Captain and let him deal with the kid. If he wants us to take the boy to the Magistrar then we won't have far to go," said another.

A brief discussion ensued, during which Barney stayed on the ground making no movement that could have caused them to suspect his motives or make them think that he was a threat. The men eventually agreed that two of their number would escort the young man to the Captain so that he could decide the fate of their captive.

Once the decision was made, the remaining men stepped back, and Barney was forced to rise to his feet before being marched off towards the Baron's castle. For a moment, as Barney stood between his escorts, he thought of using the small dagger that André had given him to assist him to escape, but he reasoned that his guards were seasoned troops; it would be suicide.

In a way, it suited Barney to be escorted as the items that he sought could only be obtained from the Duke's men and, while being escorted, he was safe from the archers above as well as the roving patrols who were on high alert and suspicious of all movement below. It did not, however, suit him to meet with the Captain. Barney's mind raced to decide on a course of action that might have a chance of success. This time he forced himself to coldly assess only the facts of his situation. He kept his thoughts devoid of emotions and assumptions.

As they drew nearer the castle they were challenged with increasing frequency. Barney also saw groups of troopers moving from house to house, bursting through doors to try to find any escapees from the previous night's battle. As his surrounds thickened with the Duke's men, Barney further regretted the decisions that had led to his capture. His reflective mood made him understand once and for all that no one solution was suited to all situations. In future, he would use his experiences to influence but not determine his decisions.

They were nearing Old Town when they entered an area that, from the number of troops out and about, was a base of operations. Barney was forcibly directed to a stairway that led up to a building which, before the Duke's occupation, had been a store. Now the raucous sounds coming from it evidenced that it contained a group of rowdy individuals who were still hyped from an adrenaline-filled night. They were cursing each other and discussing the merits of what they had done or not done with all the bravado and gusto of survivors of battle. Some short distance away Barney could also hear an armourer plying his trade.

His captors pushed him up the steps to the door of the building just as the door was flung open and a man was thrown through it. He sailed close to Barney and landed in the dirt of the road. A big muscular man appeared in the doorway.

"I said, go sleep it off!" he shouted as he wiped his hands on his greasy apron.

"My money is as good as anyone's. I've got good drinking time left."

Two other soldiers slipped past the giant in the doorway and gently restrained the evictee between them. "He meant no trouble. Lost a good friend last night, is all."

The man at the door shrugged his shoulders and went back inside.

As Barney and his captors entered the tavern, the stench of stale ale and unwashed bodies assailed Barney's senses and it was all he could do not to throw up. His good eye needed time to adjust to the tavern's dim light, but he was pushed forward without any regard for what he might need. He was directed towards a table that was set against the back wall around which, even with the packed room, there was empty space, as if an invisible barrier kept the revellers at bay.

Barney was propelled forward into the crush of bodies, serving as a makeshift ram to create space between the tavern's patrons. As he neared the table, one of his escorts cleared his throat and called out from behind him, "Excuse me sir, but we have orders to bring this boy to you."

The four men at the table turned to look at them. In that instant, Barney realised that one of his greatest fears had come true. The red-haired Captain from Marydale, whose face now bore the mark of a fresh cut that would become a scar from his right temple to his chin, had rejoined the fight from his time in Marydale. This was the same man who had viciously assaulted Tom and Maggie on that fateful day when they had driven their wagon into Marydale and the same man who had bet that he would die. Quickly Barney lowered his head to avoid the man's eyes.

"Step forward then. What is it that is so important that you would disrupt my meal?"

"Beggin' your pardon, sir--" began Barney.

"Do I know you, boy?"

"I... I doubt that, m'lord," stammered Barney, as he felt the man's searching eyes bore into the top of his head.

One of the table's other occupants sniggered at Barney's deference to the Captain. He was silenced by a glare that conveyed intimate details of the Captain's unspoken threat.

"Raise your eyes to mine," came the demand.

Barney raised his head and his good eye ever so slowly to meet those of the red-haired Captain.

The Captain let out a loud guffaw, "That shiner is one of the best that I have ever seen; been in a brawl, I see. I'm sure I've seen you before. It'll come to me. Speak up!"

Barney had disliked the dimness of the tavern when he had first entered, but now he welcomed the low light and, despite the pain and discomfort, he was thankful for his black eye and his bruised and swollen face. He stammered the list of herbs and medicinal supplies that Lucy had once given to him and added a few others that he had heard her mention before seeking permission for them to be retrieved from Marydale.

"Permission granted," said the Captain. Barney watched as one of the minions at the table hastily scribbled the order before the Captain sealed it by splashing candle wax on the parchment and then pressing his ring in the wax. The Captain tossed the parchment on the table before dropping his sword beside it.

"Take this parchment and present it if you are challenged. On your way, drop my sword off to be sharpened. Out of the door and turn right. Tell the armourer that I'll pick it up shortly, so it had better be ready. Then go and tell the healers that you have my permission to gather what you need."

As Barney leaned forward to take the sword, the Captain evilly grinned at him, "And try not to get killed on your way back."

The men at the table laughed. Barney heard one mutter to another, "Bet you five silvers that some trigger-happy archer makes certain that he doesn't make it."

Barney took the sword by the tip of the blade and pulled the sword across the table. When the sword was near enough, he spun it around so that he was able to take its hilt. The Captain stared at Barney, trying to look past his swollen face that still carried some of the soot and dirt that had been rubbed into it on the previous evening. Frowning, he sought to brush aside the fog in his mind resulting from his lack of sleep and the substantial amount of ale that he had drunk. The boy before him looked familiar and for some reason, the bet on the archer taking the boy's life meant something to him.

Without waiting a moment more, Barney seized the sword by its hilt before turning and pushing through the tavern's throng of patrons towards the door.

At the Captain's bidding, Barney's escorts stayed to have a drink on his tab. Barney wondered whether the Captain was being generous or perhaps permitting more time for bets to be placed on his fate.

Once Barney had left the tavern, he felt like every eye in the world was looking at him, waiting for him to do something out of the ordinary, waiting for him to drop his pretence. For some peculiar reason, Barney realised that he felt guilty at his deception.

He was troubled by his guilt because it was both unreasonable and illogical. His deception of the Captain was entirely reasonable. He had used his intelligence to secure a signed document from his enemy. He should be patting his own back in congratulations. He shook his head fiercely. He had casually and intentionally used lies and deceit to take advantage of those about him to secure his position. His manipulation of the circumstances was something that he should be proud of, but it ran contrary to everything that he had been taught and everything that he had been brought up to respect.

He was alive when he should be dead, but he was alienating who he had been and who he had been brought up to be. His parents' disappointment with his justification for his actions mingled with his own. If he were to look at his reflection, he was not sure who or what he would see. Logic, his companion and friend, was leaving him; everything was uncertain and everything was changing with such rapidity that it was burdening him with mental and physical adaptations that were threatening to subjugate who he believed he was. He stopped and held his hand to a wall as a wave of dizziness and nausea threatened to overwhelm him. He found the pawn in his pocket and gripped it tightly, searching for the comfort that up until now the game had always given him.

Eventually Barney calmed himself. There was no going back. He had to embrace the consequences of his actions and his decisions.

CHAPTER

SIXTEEN

———— ✦ ————

Despite his desire to be away from the area as quickly as possible, Barney resolved to find the armourer, who he correctly assumed was currently busy meeting demands to repair chain mail, remove dents from helmets and shields and generally work at completing a thousand tasks to enable the Duke's army to be ready for their next engagement.

He followed the din of metal being worked and the black smoke rising from the forges and found the armourer working with another two men in a confined area not far from the tavern. All three of them were plying their trade beneath a cacophony of sound and Barney wondered how they were not deaf.

The armourer, a large smithy, clad in a leather apron and holding a red-hot sword that he had just removed from a roaring furnace with a pair of tongs, glanced up as Barney

159

approached. He bellowed, "No more for the moment, lad. Take it elsewhere!"

The other smithies didn't even glance up. One continued to grind a blade and the other. The other grimly hammered his anvil, causing it to sing the ageless song of worked metal.

"Belongs to the Captain of the Guard, sir. Said he'll be wanting to pick it up soon."

The armourer looked from Barney to the molten metal, which would need reheating if he didn't work it soon. Barney could see both annoyance and acceptance in the man's features beneath the beaded sweat. He nodded at Barney, "I'll do that next then. Leave it on the bench and be off with you."

Barney placed the sword on the centre of the bench. The smithy returned to his work. He had already dismissed the presence of the lad while, in his mind, he was reordering the list of work in his head. Barney managed to remove two coats of chain mail, two cloaks and a helmet and a flask from a pile awaiting collection as he slipped away. The dagger that André had provided him remained hidden within his clothes, undrawn and unused. He was glad that was the case. The smiths had simply been doing their job and were not his enemy.

As he walked away, he realised that this was the first time he had ever stolen anything. Once again, he struggled with guilt. He accepted the need but wondered at the ramifications of his actions on the smithy and the soldiers to whom the equipment belonged.

Barney entered one end of a short alley as a young lad in work clothes, carrying a heavy burden. He exited from the other end as a rather diminutive soldier of the Duke, wearing two mail coats, a helmet and two cloaks. It was heavy and hot.

Head held high, he strode along the centre of the road back towards the edge of town, acknowledging the occasional trooper as he walked with a nod or a wave of his hand. He acted as though he belonged and had a reason for being there. To run would have attracted attention, but to walk in uniform with purpose in a town in which men had died the previous night and where men were conducting searches for fugitives was to hide in plain sight.

Twice he saw men on horseback leading dozens of others on house-to-house searches. Three times he was passed by troopers carrying wounded comrades. Each time, he perspired more; each time his heart beat faster and each time he resisted the urge to run. He paused only once to quench his thirst and fill the flask.

Despite his disguise he was still surprised that none of the Duke's men challenged him. Knowing that time was short, he took the most direct route back to the house where Shine and André were.

When he arrived, his expectation of being challenged came to fruition. As he opened the door, André roughly grabbed him. As Barney lay on the floor with the tip of a sword resting against his throat, he decided, with all the wisdom of hindsight, that it would have been better to have removed his helmet, knocked, called out or given some sort of signal before he entered. It would have prevented the new bruises that he knew would colour his arm and his back purple. He held his hands out wide in a gesture of surrender and watched recognition flicker in André's eyes as he realised who Barney was.

"Sorry about that," said André as he sheathed his sword and held out his hand to help Barney to his feet.

"My fault," responded Barney as he stripped off the outer layer of his clothing and passed the flask to them.

"What happened to your face?"

Barney grimaced. "I took it for granted."

André and Shine had done well in his absence. They had found some material and ingeniously fashioned a hammock from discarded hessian that they attached to a long length of wood. The boy lay face down on it, with his head tilted to one side. Barney's bow was tucked in beside him. When both ends of the length of wood were picked up the boy would be cocooned, and therefore unable to be seen easily.

André relieved Barney of one of the cloaks and one of the chain mail suits. He left Barney with the helmet as it effectively disguised his age. Shine, at their insistence, worked hard to change her appearance. Much to her disgust, she refreshed the dust and soot on her face and then rubbed ash into her hair so that it was flecked with grey. Finally, she dressed in a cloak and draped herself with a shawl, both of which were fashioned from old cloth that she had found in the house. When she walked with a stoop, using her staff as a walking stick, her appearance aged dramatically. To Barney she now looked more like an old crone. Her youthful and attractive figure was hidden; however, when Barney complimented her, she held the palm of her hand to his face and threatened to strike him with her staff if he made any further comment.

The boy was not moving; his breathing was shallow; his lips were dry and he was not responsive when André and Barney picked up each end of the length of wood. With Shine shuffling behind them and the boy swaying in his cocoon, they left the house.

They walked from the town without looking back.

As they approached the aid station, the true toll of the night's fighting was revealed by the number of casualties waiting to be treated. All the healers looked tired and distressed as they bustled about but, for all the sense of disorder, the natural state of the army had, by the time that the companions arrived, defaulted to order, based on discipline and hierarchy.

Their small party was challenged as they came to the perimeter of the aid station by a tall and officious sentry. He demanded to see the wounded individual. When he pulled aside the material, he saw the legs and back of a person who was not an adult but rather a child.

"Why would you bring a child here, even if he is wounded?" he demanded. "And who is this hag?"

Barney stiffened. "Cap'n don't like her being called a hag. Says it's disrespectful, he does."

The sentry paused at the unusual response to his challenge.

"Cap'n likely to take issue with you."

"Captain?"

"...of the Guard. You know – big fella with red hair and a mean temper."

The sentry swallowed hard, "So, what of the child?"

"Her son. His servant. Sharpens the Cap'n's sword, he does. We was ordered to fetch him here so our duty now be done."

Barney spat on the ground and motioned to André, and they lowered the stretcher.

Tension and indecision emanated from the sentry whose hand moved to the pommel of his sword.

Shine wailed into the silence.

The sentry shook his head and recovered his composure enough to say, "My orders are that this camp is for our injured only, so you will stay with them until I can clear things up.

"See the row back there. The dead. Take him near there. If a healer can spare the time to see him, well and good. If not, then you won't have far to take him when he's dead. If she stays, you stay. And shut her up!"

Barney muttered darkly under his breath and motioned to André that they should head towards the back row of casualties which was, coincidentally, the closest point in the camp to the steep slope that would take them out of the valley.

They placed their burden down on the grass and sat next to it. André looked longingly at the line of trees, "We can leave him here. He is going to die anyway. As soon as it gets dark, we make for the tree line."

When Barney pointed out that they had all agreed that they would only leave the boy once they had secured help for him, Shine stood and shuffled towards the main hospital tent to where a group of men were standing.

"What is she doing?" hissed André, as he stood to go after her.

"Wait. Stop." Barney responded, placing a restraining hand on André's arm.

Barney understood where Shine was heading. Sure enough, she stopped in front of the tall, balding Healer from Marydale. At first he was dismissive, but when she took hold of his arm and said something further to him, he looked shocked enough to listen.

Eventually, the Healer waved her away and Shine came back. By this time André was infuriated and he let his feelings show. Shine said nothing. She glared back fiercely, with an eyebrow raised. Her gaze was enough to silence him. They sat in uncomfortable silence for a short time until the Healer came over to them.

The Healer instantly recognised both Barney and André. Nodding to them, he moved the material aside and glanced down at the prone figure. All colour drained from his face.

Wide-eyed, he looked at the three of them. "Is this your idea of a joke? Have you any idea of the danger that you all are in? Not to mention the danger you have now placed me and my family in?"

All three of them stared blankly back at him.

"Surely you know who he is?"

As one they shook their heads.

"Keep him face down. In fact, cover his face. Claim he has burns, if you're asked. I'll do what I can for him and then you must all leave. You cannot risk being here and you cannot risk leaving him here. How dare you get me involved!"

Shine hid the boy's face beneath her cloak as André wrapped the boy's head with some of the bandages the Healer had brought with him. André left only enough space for the boy's eyes to observe his surroundings if he awoke, while ensuring his nose and mouth had sufficient room for him to breathe.

Barney put a hand on the Healer's shoulder, stopping him for the moment, and said, "What are you talking about? Who is he?"

The Healer looked at him with astonishment. Then he realised Barney was in earnest, "You truly don't know, do you?"

Barney shook his head.

"The silk shirt didn't give you pause? Did you really believe that a peasant or a servant could afford to wear silk? Surely you suspected something?"

Barney frowned as he tried to solve the puzzle.

The Healer sighed, "You have what this whole battle – this siege – is about. You have the King's son. If he dies, the King will forever hunt us all and his revenge will be terrible. If he lives, the Duke will hunt you. And if he finds out that I helped you, he will kill me. This is a fine mess that you have got us all into."

Shine and Barney blanched. André grimaced as he recalled how he had used the Prince as a human missile.

Barney, Shine and André watched in silence as the Healer went to work. At first, the Healer's hands shook, but then, as his professionalism took over, he worked with the efficient and swift movements of someone who was well practised in repairing the human body. He sweated profusely as he worked to free the arrow in a way that would not cause the boy any permanent disability.

Barney's eyes met those of his companions and he realised that they were all fighting the same sense of nausea.

The Healer cut away some of the Prince's tissue and exposed as much of the arrowhead as possible to see whether it was barbed or smooth. The Healer was concerned about the amount of blood that the Prince had already lost. His soft and shallow heartbeat warned the Healer that he hadn't much time.

After establishing that the arrow did not have a barbed tip, he cautiously removed it before sewing the sides of the wound together with the same type of catgut that Barney had seen his mother use to repair clothes. When he had finished, the Healer left for a short time before returning with a poultice that he smeared over the wound before binding his work with a cleanish strip of cloth.

Assuming they would take the Prince with them, the Healer handed Barney a small tub containing the remainder of the poultice, together with some fresh strips of cloth. After giving Barney brief instructions regarding their use, he concluded by saying, "I have done all I can. He needs rest and good care, and you must get water into him. If I don't go now, the Duke's soldiers will come to see what I have been doing. Good luck."

"Wait, one more thing," said Barney.

The Healer was clearly annoyed at the delay, but as Barney explained why they wanted to move the boy closer to the forest, he saw the benefit of them all leaving as soon as possible. The Healer pointed to some hastily dug graves adjacent to the last line of dead, as he shouted, "Take him over there. If he dies, bury him with the rest."

Again, they moved the boy, this time a little more gingerly; they were not quite sure what to do with a prince. Being common folk, none of them had ever seen a prince, let alone cared for one.

"So, what do we do now?" asked André.

"We'll have to take him with us," replied Barney.

"How can you possibly say that? We are untrained in healing, and I might know how a sword is wielded, but the Duke will send his best after us. You might feel good about standing between the Duke and the King, but I don't feel like being a bug that is squashed underfoot because I am an inconvenience."

Barney well understood André's point of view, but he realised that André was not seeing the bigger picture. He saw that Shine was waiting for his response.

He quickly weighed up the situation and then responded with as little emotion as possible. "Didn't you hear the Healer? If we hand the boy to the Duke and he harms him, who do you think it will be easier for the King to wreak his vengeance on? The Duke or us? We would be the scapegoats. Despite the King knowing who is at fault politically, it will be the likes of us who get the blame. If we simply abandon the Prince, then sooner or later the King's agents will trace the Prince from the castle to this camp and discover our decision to leave him. If he dies because of lack of care, then the King will blame both the Healer and us. If we want to survive, then there is only one way out of this for us."

"Which is?"

"We hand the Prince to the King and remove ourselves from the feud."

André shook his head, "You got us into this--"

"And right at this very moment, we can say with honesty to the King that not only did we save the Prince beneath the wall, but we got him to medical attention as promptly as we could."

André stared at Barney. Shine grasped André's forearm as she spoke, "André, we don't have a choice. I don't want to spend the rest of my life looking over my shoulder, waiting for those loyal to the King to find us. I won't sneak around the forest with you as an outlaw hiding from everyone and everything that I know. Listen to Barney. If there was another choice, this would be a discussion, but we have no choice. I couldn't look Lucy in the eye if I walked away from this injured boy, so the decision has been made for us. Right now, we are his only hope. We need to do this, but we can't do it without you."

Barney could see indecision pulsing through André's features. He could tell that André wanted to run. Some part of Barney agreed with that notion. The odds of them presenting a living prince to the King were long.

André said nothing as they carried the boy to the end of the line of the dead. They placed the Prince on the ground, as close as possible to the slope that they would have to climb before reaching the tree line. They were as far as they could get from the camp without arousing suspicion.

"I'll help you on one condition," said André, as he lowered himself to the grass.

"And that is?"

"If we succeed, we never see you again."

"André! No!"

Barney thought of the danger that his decisions had placed them in. He looked at Shine before returning his gaze to André. "Agreed."

CHAPTER

EIGHTEEN

——— ✦ ———

From the town, on the far side of the camp, riders appeared escorting a wagon. A large, barred cage was fixed to the bed of the wagon. In the middle of the cage sat two or three troopers wearing the colours of the Baron. The Duke's soldiers jeered at the wagon as it passed through the throng gathered along its path. The numbers were so great that Barney doubted whether the wagon's escort would deter the Duke's soldiers from attacking. Apprehension filled Barney as the crowd became more vocal and objects were hurled at the captives.

The wagon was led towards an area adjoining the main hospital tent that Barney had not previously noticed. Patrolling guards paced around the exterior of the tent. As the wagon approached, the guards formed up into a corridor to ensure that the captives could be safely escorted inside, away from the mob. At least one of the captives appeared to be injured. As the crowd surged forward, the guards drew their swords in warning. Heeding the threat, the crowd gradually began to disperse.

The sun was beginning to lower itself to the horizon when the first screams from the tent rent the air, imparting to all the knowledge that the Duke's torturers had begun to ply their trade. Some of those who had been in the crowd around the wagon gave a cheer. Although Barney was quite a distance away, he could hear the sobs of agony that followed the anguished screams.

When one of the screaming troopers fell silent, Barney watched as the Healer was summoned inside the tent. When he reappeared a short time later, he was followed by two men carrying a body. Together they headed towards the graveyard.

Barney and the others sat together in silence in the lengthening shadows, watching as the men approached. The body was deposited, without ceremony, into the mass grave not far from where they sat. Barney watched as one of the bearers paused to spit on the corpse. The companions and their charge were ignored.

The Healer delayed leaving. Barney reached for his bow and partially slid his knife from his belt. Something was not quite right.

The Healer did not come to them but stayed close to the grave. He appeared to be taking notes. As he wrote he did not look at them and when he spoke, it was as if he was softly addressing the deceased, "This man died because he couldn't tell them what happened to the Prince. The Duke believes the Prince might have tried to escape from the Baron's castle, but he doesn't know for sure. At this very moment his troops are conducting door-to-door searches throughout Landsend.

They might burn the whole of the town to the ground if they don't find him. They have called for bloodhounds, trackers and for something to scent the hounds. You need to go now! I will be of no more assistance to you."

The Healer strode off without another word. Barney turned to the others, and they urgently began to plan their next move while wishing with all of their might that the sun would set just a little bit faster.

They were deep in discussion when a group of seven cavalry arrived. The riders were armed to the teeth. The red-haired Captain of the Guard rode in front of them, leading them on. He had finally recalled the old farmer, his wife and their son and he now knew why he'd experienced a sense of déjà vu when they had placed bets on the boy evading the town's archers. And now he wanted answers.

As soon as Barney realised who the horsemen were, he regretted not warning the Healer about the story he had spun to the Captain. Now he could only hope that the Healer could somehow avoid suspicion. With the arrival of the Captain, Barney knew that they were out of options and in grave danger.

Darkness had not banished the final light of the day and the three companions knew that there was a risk in moving the Prince; however, the circumstances had now changed dramatically. The threat to all of them was imminent. They had to act before events overtook them.

Barney slipped away first, taking with him his bow and remaining arrows. Stooping low, he quickly covered the distance to where the steep slope of the valley's side rose from the valley floor. When he was at the foot of the slope, he knelt on one knee and placed the quiver with his arrows to his left and the bow on the ground to his right. He hoped that the gathering shadows would cover all of their movements.

Barney watched as André, in one smooth motion, stood and heaved the boy, who was now trussed up like a sack, up and onto his shoulder. With Shine pointing the way, they moved unhurriedly towards Barney.

They had just started up the slope when Barney heard a sentry issue a challenge from the camp. André pretended he hadn't heard. Barney was now alone, between his friends and the Duke's army.

More shouting ensued. Barney saw the Captain take notice. André leant into the slope and pressed on. It would soon be time for Barney to follow suit. Moments before he did, the Captain summoned one of his riders to him. After a brief discussion, the man spurred his horse towards André.

Barney's friends were still struggling up the slope and they were in the open. Barney was concerned. He'd never shot a moving target; he knew the theory but not the practice. He notched an arrow, keeping his movements slow. The bowstring slotted into place.

The rider was concentrating on the two figures moving towards the tree line, straining his eyes in the dimming light to keep them in sight. Barney's movements were, for the moment, slight enough to elude the periphery of the rider's vision. The rider's agitation was growing. It was obvious that André was ignoring him. He spurred his horse onwards.

As the rider came closer and closer to Barney, he knew that he had only one chance. He shuddered at the consequences of failure before he pushed the thought from his mind.

From the direction of the town, there came the sound of trumpets. Startled, the rider looked around. As he did,

Barney took his chance and stood. He squinted with his one good eye and drew before releasing the drawstring. The arrow flew into the man's side at almost point-blank range.

Time seemed to slow. In the town, the Baron's troops streamed from the castle's open gates towards the scene of the previous night's battle, searching for the Prince. The Captain and the rest of the Duke's men had all been distracted by the sound of the trumpets. Barney's target started to slip from his saddle.

The horse smelt blood and prepared for battle by rearing high in the air to challenge the unseen enemy. It was the rearing of the horse that attracted the Captain's attention. As André made it safely to the trees, the Captain caught sight of Barney fleeing up the slope towards the tree line. Barney was immediately the centre of his attention.

The Captain cursed and dug his spurs into his horse. He charged towards Barney, calling for his men to follow. Around the Captain, the Duke's officers were responding to the trumpets by shouting orders to the Captain and his men as they sped by. The officers wanted all able-bodied men in the vicinity to respond to the Baron's challenge by rushing to the castle gates.

Barney kept running up the slope towards the safety of the trees.

Further orders were shouted, followed by threats. These at first were ignored by the Captain. He wanted, no, he needed to chase down the figure who he believed to be Barney. More orders were hurled at him to remind him of his duty. As the Captain of the Guard, he was needed to lead the Duke's men to victory.

Finally, a member of the Duke's court threatened to charge the Captain with desertion. Begrudgingly, with no other option, and not wanting to face a death sentence, the Captain hauled on the reins of his horse. In despair, he motioned his men on towards the fleeing figure and watched as they stretched their horses into a gallop before he spun his mount on the spot. He viciously drove his spurs into his horse's flanks and charged back towards the castle.

The Captain's men were quickly narrowing the gap. As Barney plunged into the tree line, the branches of the undergrowth pushed against him, resisting his flight. He could hear his pursuers calling to each other as they hurriedly dismounted. Onwards he ran. He needed a clear line of sight to use his bow. To distract his pursuers, he planned to fire and then disappear before repeating his efforts.

Barney ran through the trees and up over the rise before crossing over a path that was barely the width of a wagon. Pausing behind a tree on the other side of the path, Barney breathed deeply in a desperate attempt to calm himself.

His heart was still racing as he notched his first arrow and waited.

NINETEEN

The rough bark of the tree was damp. Barney could feel it through his clothing. His run up the slope had been difficult. The violent spasms of his breathing were testament to his exertion. He could barely resist sinking to his haunches. Barney could see nothing of his companions. He felt alone, utterly alone, and it occurred to him how true that statement was. Shine had André and Lucy and he had... no one. Barney shook his head to clear his thoughts. He had already bought Shine time and now he had the ability to buy her more. Shine would escape – he would make sure of it.

Behind him, he could hear shouting and the sounds of his pursuers pushing through the undergrowth. Soon they would be upon him. He fixed upon his plan and marked out the next tree. Shoot. Move. Shoot. Repeat. Best to keep it simple: fewer things that could go wrong. He could feel the presence of the pawn in his pocket but didn't dare remove either hand from his bow to grasp it. Instead, he moved the heel of his hand to brush against it. With singular intent he peered around the trunk of the tree.

The Captain's men crested the rise and ran across the path. Barney stepped out from behind the tree and fired.

The shot was rushed and affected by his shaking hands. The arrow passed to the right of the lead man who didn't even pause. He was supposed to have paused or taken cover! There was no time for Barney to move and no time for another shot. The man crashed into Barney, knocking him from his feet. His bow flew from his grasp. A knife was pressed against his throat.

"I remember you. You're that boy the Captain let go in Marydale. I would dearly like to kill you, but the Captain wants to personally deal with you. Where are your companions?"

"I... don't know."

In response, the trooper's punch broke Barney's nose.

"Not so pretty now, are you?" Five men surrounded Barney. After being forced to his feet, he was punched in his stomach with enough force to drive the breath from his body. He collapsed on the ground before being hauled, once again, to his feet. A sword tip was pressed against his back, forcing him towards the camp.

The tears in Barney's eyes, resulting from the punch to his nose, blurred the vision from his one remaining good eye and blood cascaded down over his chin. Wearily, with shoulders slumped, he accepted his fate and began to retrace his steps towards the last of the trees.

As Barney approached the final trees, it was to his advantage that he was shorter than his captor. The height difference left the upper part of his captor's body exposed. Barney heard the whispering sound of an arrow passing above him. The man holding the sword to his back died instantly as the arrow's steel tip burrowed into his forehead.

A dark shadowy figure stepped out from behind a tree in front of them. He fired another arrow and downed another man. Bertrand had returned to meet them as promised.

The three remaining troopers charged towards the threat, intent on revenge. Bertrand dropped his bow and drew a short sword. He then planted his feet firmly on the ground. Nothing about him exhibited any intention to retreat.

André and Shine broke cover to either side of the remaining troopers as they charged towards Bertrand.

Shine swung her staff with all of her strength, horizontally, into the man's face. He had no time to sidestep the attack, which knocked him from his feet. As he fell to the ground, he lost consciousness.

At the same time André slid out from behind a tree, dropping into a crouch that was so low that his left knee brushed the ground behind his right foot. As his taller opponent went to overrun his position André slipped beneath the trooper's sword. André braced himself and thrust his entire body forward. Using his sword like a spear, he impaled the man through his chest to the hilt of his sword. The trooper collapsed over André's shoulders in a bloodied heap.

The remaining trooper, distracted by his comrades' fates, realised that with André and Shine to his flank, he now had no choice but to fight his way past the short, dishevelled man before him. He knew his reach with his sword would be far greater than that of his adversary, who stood unmoving before him, preventing him from making his way back to the Duke's encampment.

The trooper reached Bertrand. To immediately overpower Bertrand, the trooper swung his weapon with all of his might. The trooper expected to brush his adversary aside. Bertrand held his ground and turned the blow aside without undue effort.

Shine, André and Barney stayed back. None of them had ever seen swordplay in its purest form, the short and sharp skirmishes of two opponents embittered by their belief in their superiority and their right to survive as they fought to be victorious in one-on-one combat.

They fought as equals, with passion and with elegant precision and a quickly found respect for each other's abilities. The display of their skill was entrancing. The two blades met in combinations of lightning-fast movement. Each sought an opening in the defences of the other and time and time again each was denied. Bertrand, at a significant disadvantage in height and therefore reach, was clearly being less aggressive and more defensive and patient than his opponent.

After the initial engagement, the two men stepped back from each other to catch their breath, taking the time to measure the stance and to consider the skill of the other before they launched themselves once more into an attack.

Finally, after what seemed an age and after each man had suffered several cuts to their torsos and arms, the trooper stumbled on the rough terrain. Seizing his chance, Bertrand swung his sword down towards the trooper. At the last possible moment, as the man raised his sword to take the blow, Bertrand changed the direction of his weapon, deftly manoeuvring his blade around that of his opponent before redirecting it to swing back towards the soldier's body, cutting deeply into his exposed side.

The man howled in pain. Bertrand drew back his sword before thrusting it forward once more to end the man's life. The light left the man's eyes as he slid, lifeless, to the ground. Bertrand collapsed to his haunches, panting for breath, his cool demeanour lost in the moment.

Barney was dazed. They had come to his rescue. They had risked everything for him. He could think of nothing to say. He sank to the ground, relieved that, for the moment, they were all precariously safe and away from the camp.

After they had briefly rested, they took their time to strip some arms from the Duke's soldiers and retrieve Barney's bow from where it had fallen.

Taking the cloaks from two of the dead, Bertrand directed André to use his sword to cut down two saplings. Then, after tying the cloaks to the saplings, they fashioned another improvised stretcher. Two other cloaks were kept for bedding to keep the Prince warm.

Barney had been surprised by Bertrand's skill with the blade. He could tell that Bertrand had received the benefit of being trained by a master of the art; however, he didn't know Bertrand well enough to tell him who the boy was, so he told the others that, for the time being, it was their secret. There was no point in telling anyone who didn't need to know, that they were responsible for the life of the King's son.

Bertrand kept guard as they made swift preparations to set off. When they were ready, Shine and André took them to the prone boy, whose face was still wrapped in bandages.

Bertrand grunted and said, "He appears badly wounded. He'll slow us down. Why take the trouble to bring him?"

Without hesitation, Barney lied. "He's my brother. We're not leaving him. We need Lucy to tend his wounds. Please take us to her as quickly as possible."

When neither Shine nor André raised any objection, Bertrand shrugged his shoulders, "So be it. He's your burden to bear, not mine."

The stretcher was cumbersome, and it was lucky for them that the Prince was young and light, but even so, balancing the stretcher on their shoulders or alternatively carrying it down at waist level took its toll. In the gathering darkness, the undergrowth of the damp forest worked to burden and then entangle any unwary leg. It was a miracle that neither stretcher-bearer sprained an ankle.

Despite his short stature, Bertrand's pace forced the three of them into a jogtrot. As they travelled, Shine took her turn at being a stretcher-bearer so Barney and André could each have short periods of rest. The terrain was far different from the route that they had taken three nights previously to approach the town. When queried, Bertrand told them that the events at the castle were causing reinforcements to be rushed from Marydale to Landsend, so it was best if they first travelled away from their destination before circling back around to where the others were hiding.

As they progressed, fatigue settled over the companions, and they became more and more irritable with each other. They snapped demands to swap from being a stretcher-bearer. Leaden feet struck objects that they would ordinarily have easily avoided. Blisters opened on their hands, feet and shoulders, and their shoulders drooped further and further with every step.

It was well past midnight when Bertrand called a halt beside a thick copse. "Press under the branches and go in as far as you can."

The low overhanging branches of several trees had meshed, creating a barrier for travel; however, when the companions pushed through to the centre of the copse, where no light reached even on the brightest of days to encourage new growth, they found a damp but surprisingly spacious hollow.

"I will stand guard while you rest," called Bertrand.

No one thought to query Bertrand about his ability to stay awake on watch. Later, Barney realised that Bertrand had preserved enough energy by not carrying the stretcher to be able to keep watch, without sleep, for the rest of the night.

When he awoke, Barney had no idea how long he'd been there. He didn't feel refreshed, but he had thrown off the worst of his shackles of tiredness. His head throbbed due to the combined effects of acute dehydration and his broken nose. His eye remained swollen shut and he could feel the squelching liquid in the blisters on his hands. Desperately needing a drink, he crawled out from beneath the trees and emerged from the undergrowth to find Bertrand sitting with his back to a nearby tree.

"Water?" he croaked.

Bertrand jerked his head. "Yonder. There's a small stream. Not far. Water is fresh. I suggest you take the time to wash your face. When you return, I have some fish and berries for you to eat. You look terrible, by the way."

Barney wondered whether he was being mocked, but when he saw, on top of some large broad leaves, the remains of a medium-sized gutted and descaled fish besides some berries, his stomach growled with such hunger that he decided not to waste any time in a pointless argument. He went to slake his thirst.

Barney quickly found the stream and drank greedily from its cool waters. He sat for a short while, considering what the day might bring. Soon, his hunger proved too distracting so, after splashing some water on his face and wiping away the worst of the dried blood, he returned to Bertrand who slid several slices of the raw fish across the leaf to him. Barney slipped the flesh between his lips and barely chewed before swallowing. The fish was tangy and had a salty flavour. The meal didn't do much more than ignite his thirst again and it did little to assuage his hunger. The berries stained his skin. After he had eaten some of them he still felt ravenous and had to stop himself from eating the entire food supply so that the others might have something.

"Your brother?" asked Bertrand.

"Alive. Lucy will take care of him."

"You've never mentioned a brother before."

Barney was immediately alert. Bertrand was suspicious.

"I'm not taking you to Lucy. Can you keep him alive?" stated Bertrand in a blunt but matter-of-fact tone.

Barney was startled at the directness of the man. "What?"

"We'll lead them directly to the camp if we head that way. Can you keep him alive?"

"No. None of us has anything but a basic knowledge of herbs and cures. Lucy received training from the Healer in Marydale. I don't know anyone else with her skill who wouldn't already be at the castle camp serving the Duke. Do you?"

"You say that only Lucy can save him?"

"I've lost the remainder of the poultice that the Healer gave me. Lucy has far more healing knowledge than anyone else in this party. She mightn't be able to save him, but she is his best and perhaps his only chance."

Bertrand stared at him as if considering whether Barney was telling the truth. In surprisingly quick time he came to a decision and nodded his head. It was as if Barney had passed some obscure test.

"I know of a safe haven and I will tell you how to find it. You'll need to get there and wait until I bring Lucy to you. Then we will travel to the capital of the Kingdom and the safety of the King's army. You must protect the Prince."

Barney gaped at the man. "How did you know?"

"I didn't know for sure, but you just confirmed my suspicions," said Bertrand with a self-satisfied smirk. "Get the others; we must leave. The Duke's advisers will probably decide soon enough that the Prince is no longer in the castle. When that happens, they will investigate strange activities. It won't be long before reports of what we did last night surface. Won't take 'em long to come looking."

Barney hesitated but he realised that he had no idea where they were or how to get to Lucy on his own. He, unfortunately, had to trust this strange little man. Besides, logically, if Bertrand had wanted to betray the Prince's location to the Duke he could have done that last night, as they slept, or when the Duke's men had caught up to Barney. He didn't know Bertrand's motives but, for whatever reason, he seemed to be on their side. The best and perhaps only way forward was to forge ahead until an alternative opportunity arose.

It didn't take long for Barney to assemble the others. They drank and ate quickly before removing the wrapping from the Prince's head so that they could try to dribble water through his dried and cracked lips.

In the time that it took them to get ready to leave, Bertrand had sketched a rough map of the area on some parchment that he had removed from his cloak. On the map, he indicated where he believed the King's army to be, where they were and the important landmarks that they would need to locate as they travelled. He assured them that they would reach the forest's edge by mid-morning. He urged them to stay away from anyone else to prevent word of their passage passing back to the Duke. He indicated the location of several streams and advised them to walk as much as possible in their waters so that the scent of their tracks would be obscured. Finally, he marked a spot, high in a mountain pass, where he assured them that they would find an old, abandoned shepherd's hut: he would meet them there in approximately two days.

"How will we know that we are travelling in the right direction while we remain amongst the trees?" asked Barney. "We got lost in the forest near Marydale and that forest wasn't as dense as this one."

Bertrand raised his eyebrow, "First, as I just said, it's mostly downhill and second, just follow the moss."

At Barney's puzzled expression Bertrand snorted, "So, the midget with attitude knows something that you do not. In this kingdom, the prevailing wind is from the north and the moss mainly grows on the southern side of the trees, so to go south, keep the moss at your backs."

Barney blushed with embarrassment and responded feebly, "I'm sorry; I shouldn't have said that... I didn't know you then... Thank you for pointing out the moss."

Bertrand grunted, turned and melted into the forest, with the beginnings of a smile playing at the corner of his lips despite the worry that coursed through his veins.

C H A P T E R

TWENTY

❖

Shine tried to make the Prince as comfortable as possible while André and Barney wrapped their hands in cloth in a vain attempt to protect them. When they were all ready, they lifted their burden from the ground. The Prince was as white as a ghost; his breathing was shallow but regular. As they walked, they took careful note of the moss on the trees and the general slope of the terrain but despite Bertrand's prediction, their pace was so slow that they failed to reach the forest's edge until well after midday.

Once again Shine helped in carrying the Prince to give each of the young men a short break. When she wasn't carrying the stretcher, she foraged for food. By the time they had finally stopped at the edge of the forest to look over the rolling hills of pasture, which appeared to have been set aside for the grazing of sheep and cattle, Shine had managed to gather a considerable quantity of fruit and berries. They stopped for a time within the shelter of the trees to savour their food, knowing that once they were out in the open, they would have to keep moving as they were likely to be spotted from a distance.

To the south, they could see the peaks of the mountain range that divided the Kingdom. They knew they had to locate a pass in that mountain range. When they studied Bertrand's map, they realised that they had only drifted slightly off course.

Shine pointed towards the distant peaks, "He marked the highest peaks on the map. It looks like we should head to the left of the tallest one."

"Agreed," responded André. "We'll be in the open the whole way."

"If we avoid using the crests of the hills and any ridge lines, we'll avoid being silhouetted," remarked Barney.

"It'll take us longer. It won't be a direct route."

"Agreed, but speed isn't everything. Better that we aren't seen. It will also mean that the terrain is flatter – might make it easier to carry the stretcher."

André grunted and thought it over but couldn't find fault with Barney's reasoning. He rose to his feet, "Well, no point waiting. Let's get on with it."

Barney sighed and moved to the foot of the stretcher. Together they crouched and picked it up. Immediately, Barney's shoulders and hands protested; he grimaced and willed himself to just take one step at a time.

TWENTY-ONE

They hadn't realised how closed in and confined that they had felt beneath the tree canopy until they stepped out from its shade. It was almost as if the bright sunlight lifted a burden from their shoulders. Once they were in the open, they looked back in the direction of the Baron's castle. They could clearly make out a thick plume of smoke that appeared to link distant dark, moody and rolling storm clouds to the ground from which the smoke rose.

That night they sheltered in a shallow cave below a ridgeline and ate all the remaining food that they had gathered.

When they'd finished they were still hungry. From where he sat, André caught sight of a lamb, "Shall we?" he queried as he reached for his knife.

Barney looked up, "Wish we could, but there is no point – we've no fuel for a fire and nothing to light a fire with."

"Surely—" began Shine.

"And if we did manage to light a fire, there's no way that it wouldn't be seen. The cave is too shallow. We'd have to spend the rest of the night and tomorrow looking out for the shepherd."

André muttered something dark under his breath and sheathed his knife, "I'll take first watch."

The next morning, as the light from the new day began to bathe the ground, they could see that the ominous clouds of the northern storm front had drawn closer to them. They could hear the faint rumble of distant thunder which was carried to them by a stiff, cool and confused breeze.

Their shelter was insufficient to provide cover from the oncoming storm and if they did stay where they were, they risked being late to their rendezvous with Bertrand and Lucy. They decided that their best option was to continue through the pastures and then up to the mountain pass where they would find shelter in the shepherd's hut.

By mid-morning, it had begun to drizzle. Flashes of lightning casually began to tear at the sky. The companions could foresee the violence that the storm would bring, and so they now travelled as fast as they could with as little rest as possible.

Shortly after the first drops of light rain fell, the wind quickened and once again changed direction. This time it blew directly from the way that they had come.

At first Barney dismissed what he heard, but when he heard it again, his blood ran cold and it was as if he was transported back to his flight from Marydale. He paused mid-stride, causing André to lurch to a stop.

André looked over his shoulder, noting Barney's ashen face, "What?"

"Don't you hear it?"

André listened for a moment. "Hear what?"

A moment later, Shine looked up at them. "Dogs?"

The next moment the wind freshened and a gust brought the clear and distinct sound to all of them. The baying of a pack of hounds. The Healer's warning was coming to fruition. They were being tracked and despite their best efforts the hounds had caught their scent.

Panicked, they looked about them. There were no trees to climb or places to hide and although the undulating landscape would obscure them from being seen from a distance, the dogs would follow their scent and eventually find them.

The companions ran! Running with a laden stretcher is, at the best of times, difficult. Running with a laden stretcher that had been carried for close to two days over all sorts of terrain, with blisters covering their hands and tiredness in their steps was almost impossible, but still, they tried.

They had no way of knowing how close the following hounds were. As the wind quickened the dogs sounded louder, but they couldn't tell whether this was because they were directly on their heels, or because the sounds of the pursuit were carried to them more quickly by the wind.

Doubt led to fear and fear led to flight. Gritting their teeth, they ran on, half looking behind them and half looking where they were going. This distraction, coupled with their confused gait, was a recipe for disaster.

Barney was carrying the rear of the stretcher when he tripped and fell forward onto it. As he fell, all of his weight pushed onto the sapling poles that André still held. One of the poles gave way. The stretcher was broken. The Prince rolled from it, into the mud that was gathering beneath their feet.

Slightly dazed, Barney looked on as André used a strip of cloth to tie the boy's hands together before he looped them over his head and lifted the Prince piggyback-style onto his back. He gestured for Shine to encircle both himself and the Prince with one of the disused cloaks that had formed the basis of the stretcher.

"Grab your bow. We need to move."

Snatching up his bow, Barney leapt to his feet and they were off, running as fast as they could away from the dogs.

Unfortunately for them, the dogs were not unfit house animals. These hounds had been bred for hunting. There was no way that Barney and his friends would ever outrun them. Indeed, the dogs' long, loping style of running simply ate the miles. If they had not been trained to stay within hearing of their master, they would have caught up with their quarry long ago.

Five experienced horsemen who had hunted with dogs all their lives travelled behind the animals. These men were the Duke's enforcers. The Captain, now freed from his duties at the castle, was leading them from the front. Publicly, they had been charged with finding the murderous deserters who had left the Duke's encampment, but privately, even though the Duke believed that the Prince remained in Landsend, the Captain had been given a description of the Prince with a promise of riches beyond measure should he bring back the Prince alive.

Despite his orders, the Captain did not really care whether the Prince was in the party that he was tracking. His orders to his enforcers were brutally simple – kill the whole party that had escaped the town but leave Barney unharmed. The Captain could think only of the vengeance that he would wreak upon Barney; the boy had escaped him three times and would not do so again. The Captain had not told his superiors of his vendetta. He had volunteered to pursue the group and bring them to justice; however, he intended to recover from his loss of face, avenge his dog and avenge his men by slowly and painfully taking Barney's life. He would not permit Barney to escape his clutches for a fourth time.

The wind continued to carry the noise of the pursuers to the fleeing party. There was no time to rest. Digging deep, they forced themselves to find levels of endurance they didn't know that they had.

They came to what looked to be a frequently used crossing at a rain-swollen stream. Leaping in, they pushed their way through the water. They waded desperately across the current. As they were about to reach the other side Barney stopped.

"Wait. Follow me! I think I know what we should do."

To leave the stream would be to immediately expose their scent to the hounds. Time to stop, contain the panic, and think. Trekking downstream was the easiest route; however, it was also the most logical direction of travel, so Barney pointed upstream.

Now it was difficult. Even close to shore the water was at waist level and pushing directly against them. It was slow going and they had no idea how near their pursuers were. It was a gamble and time was against them.

The rain had begun to fall heavily by the time the riders reached the ford. Midstream, the waters had risen to about the height of the belly of a standing horse. The Captain directed some of his hounds to swim to the other side. Once they had crawled from the water, they walked in circles, seeking the scent of their quarry. Eventually, it became obvious that they had failed to find the trail and they looked to the Captain for direction. Glancing at the sky, the Captain muttered a profanity under his breath and then, whistling to his enforcers, he ordered half of the remaining dogs to go to the far bank with three of his men. Once they were in place, he signalled for both parties to set off downstream in search of the fugitives.

The Captain was desperate to find some clue before the storm front engulfed them.

Upriver, Barney had heard the dogs reach the ford and he realised that they had got lucky. He urged the others to push on until they could no longer bear the force of the swift water. They then left the swollen stream using a muddy game trail that headed generally in the right direction.

The Prince was passed to Barney by André. He immediately appreciated the difficulty that André had had to contend with. The Prince was a deadweight and that weight pressed down directly onto Barney's lower back, which was already beginning to protest. How André had not fallen in the waters was a tribute to his strength. Despite his discomfort, Barney vowed silently to himself to keep the Prince as long as possible because both André and Shine were able to defend the party in combat with their sword and staff. With a wet bowstring, his arrows would be unlikely to travel with any force towards their intended target.

They moved on and the rain fell heavier. Lightning split the sky and thunder shook the earth. The storm in all of its fury settled over them.

There was no hiding from the rain. It soaked them to the core. The game trail led them towards the rugged mountain range that stood between them and the gentler pastures of the southern part of the Kingdom.

Barney focussed his memory on the map that Bertrand had drawn for them, counting off the references to the specific landmarks that Bertrand had noted. The rain obscured much of the landscape, but in the darkness the lightning acted as a conduit that created snapshots – brief paintings of moments in time – that enabled him to scan for the details that he required.

In all, there were five features that he needed to look for. The first was easy to find: three pillars of rock rising from the bottom of the slope of the range. The pillars were not far from the game trail. As he left it, he didn't notice André go to question him or Shine placing a restraining hand on André's shoulder. He didn't realise that by this time, André and Shine were completely disorientated and totally reliant on him. In truth, it was only the confidence of his steps that kept either of the others going.

When they reached the pillars, Barney looked to his left and waited once more for the lightning to reveal the landscape. He made out the partially obscured shape of the white trunk of a long-dead tree moments before it disintegrated into a million pieces when lightning struck it. The resultant boom of thunder made them all flinch and duck as if to avoid the sound. Resolutely, with Shine and André in tow, Barney strode towards where the tree had been standing.

The stump of the tree, despite the volume of water that was falling upon it, was still smouldering when they reached it.

The third landmark was much harder to find – the mouth of a cave high up on the mountain. They were to head towards it and then stop when they came to a stand of bushes.

The problem was that the mouth of the cave was dark. While lightning revealed snapshot after snapshot of the mountain, it was difficult to distinguish between light and shade in the short amount of time afforded by the lightning strikes.

Barney settled into a pattern. He stared at a spot with his one good eye and then when he was sure that the mouth of the cave was not there, he moved his gaze slightly before refocusing his concentration. He dismissed the weight of the Prince and forced himself not to duck from the thunder. He stood so still that Shine wondered for a moment whether he was in shock.

Barney didn't realise that he was shivering intensely until he heard teeth chattering. He was relieved when André and Shine worked to remove the Prince from his back, but he didn't allow himself to move. Suddenly his mind, not his eye, registered a difference in the colour of terrain up high and to his left. He waited for three more flashes to be sure before he lifted his arm and pointed. He didn't bother to attempt to shout over the storm. He kept his eyes on his target and moved off, sensing the others following his lead.

Every now and again he would lose sight of the cave and he would stop and wait until he regained its position before he strode off. His focus was so myopic that he found the stand of bushes by stepping into its branches.

Once he realised where he was, he turned until he caught sight of two trees whose branches were intertwined from the height of an average man. He pointed between them. They were going up a steep incline now and the ground beneath their feet was made slippery by running water.

When he reached the trees, Barney made out a cleft in the rock behind them. He didn't pause. He strode towards it. And then into it, the others following close on his heels.

Almost immediately, Barney was relieved that they were away from the direct effect of the rain, but still they were not safe.

Water cascaded down the sides of the cleft from the cliff of the mountain on one side and the steep hills on the other. The cleft had acted as a natural drain for aeons. It directed and concentrated the flow of water. Over time that flow of water had eroded the path on which they now stood. The speed of the water was enough to make each step perilous and on several occasions each of them slipped over and bloodied another part of their person.

The companions' lips were blue, and their limbs were losing feeling, but they stayed in the torrent of water. Rounding a bend, they found themselves in a flat spacious area: behind them stood the imperious stone cliffs of the mountain while steep grassy rolling hills stretched out before them. At the foot of the hills was the rudest and roughest looking hut that any of them had ever seen. To get to it, they had to venture into the deluge of falling rain again.

From the exterior 'shabby' was a very kind description. None of its walls were the same height; they looked solid but brittle. The wood appeared to have deteriorated over time to such an extent that it was a wonder that the walls still stood. Strips of bark were flapping in the wind. The bark had been tugged from the walls and roof by Mother Nature's desire to clear the land for trees and plants to grow. Oddly, there were no visible windows. Shutters appeared to have survived, boarding up the structure from the wind. That the roof was still in place appeared to be either a tribute to its builders or just lucky.

Barney attempted to grit and thereby quieten his chattering teeth without success. They had no choice. They had to get protection from the rain. Straightening his shoulders and standing tall, Barney led the others towards the hut. The rain seemed to intensify as if it were seeking to deny them whatever little shelter that the hut might offer.

Barney squelched onto the veranda and reached with his shaking hand for the door handle. He didn't knock. There was no point. The cacophony of noise created by the storm would render any attempt to knock useless. He simply pushed down on the handle and hoped that any occupant would understand their desperate need for shelter. The door swung open to reveal a darkened room.

They left the door open so that the lightening could provide them with brief moments of illumination to enable them to peer into the darkness. They discovered an oil lamp near the door and beside it a tinderbox. André unceremoniously dumped the Prince on the floor, seized the lamp and the tinderbox and took it to a nearby table. His companions heard him set it down before striking the fire steel and muttering to himself as sparks cascaded down upon the plant fibres that were in the tinderbox.

"Shut the damn door! If I can do this with my eyes shut, I can do it in the dark!"

Barney closed the door. Instantly the sound of the storm abated and for a moment he was disorientated – The silence was almost deafening.

Once. Twice. Thrice, André struck the fire steel. A dull redness collected in the plant fibres. Gently, André blew on it. A tiny flame rose and then, using a wooden splint, he transferred the flame to the lamp.

Shine and Barney hadn't realised that they had been holding their breath. As the lamp began to emit light, Barney latched the door.

The state of the interior of the hut belied its external appearance. The walls and roof were evidently watertight. The inside of the hut, although small, was surprisingly clean and organised. The beams of wood that supported the structure were sturdy despite their apparent age. The boards that formed the walls that had looked so mismatched, forlorn and old from the outside were stout and finished with a preciseness that was totally at odds with the hut's external appearance. Shelving held sealed jars containing what looked like dried meat and fruit. Other supplies were stored in containers that blended into the walls or formed part of the furniture, such as a chest beneath the benches that formed the seats for the table. Someone had gone to a great deal of trouble to disguise the appearance of the hut.

There was no one home. They appeared to have the place to themselves.

The companions shivered uncontrollably. Their skin, overly wet, was shrivelled and pale and ready to peel should it be rubbed by anything other than the lightest touch. With little discussion, Barney and Shine formed a small pile of kindling in the fireplace and transferred the lamp's flame to it. At least they would be able to warm and dry themselves. There was no way that the light of the fire would be seen from the outside and any smoke would be dispersed by the wind almost before it left the chimney but, more than anything, despite any danger from being caught by their pursuers, if they sickened as a result of their cold and wet conditions they would be unable to flee or fight for their lives. They needed to get warm quickly. Better to be alive and warm than shivering and ill while attempting to avoid pursuers who might never come.

Barney and Shine stripped the Prince of his clothing, wrapped him in a blanket and lay him down on the floor as close as possible to the fire. André busied himself by adding fuel to the fire. The Prince's breathing was shallow, and he made no sound or movement.

Once they had settled the Prince, the companions removed their own clothing and dried themselves on whatever material that they could find before wrapping themselves in blankets and joining the Prince by the fire. As they huddled together, the flickering flames took hold. At first, they only provided the companions with light to see and enough warmth to hold the cold at bay, but thankfully it didn't take too long before the tendrils of heat caused the cool temperature to retreat to the furthest reaches of the cabin.

Outside, the world tore itself apart. The party of men by the stream was now separated by floodwaters. They had hobbled their horses and were huddled with their dogs in whatever shelter they could find. In the distance, the fighting at the Baron's castle ceased as the madness of men bowed before the storm. The only movement was a man on an unfamiliar horse, with a sullen girl riding in front of him wrapped beneath his cloak, desperately trying to find a way through the mud and water to reach Barney and his friends.

TWENTY-TWO

When the hut had borrowed enough of the warmth of the fire to make it pleasant, André moved the Prince to a bed while Shine and Barney located the necessary supplies in the hut to make a hearty broth. As they watched the broth come to the boil they all salivated. It was their first hot meal since they had left Lucy, Tom and Maggie in the safety of their camp beside the stream. Even though some of the ingredients wouldn't usually have been found on the same plate, it tasted as though they were consuming a feast that had been cooked under the direction of a master chef. The poor shepherd was going to have to resupply his hut after they had completed their stay.

After they had finished their meal, the three companions slumped on the floor, partly dozing, as they watched the flames consuming the wood before them. With a clear head, Barney allowed his good eye to dance around the hut. Under close inspection the hut revealed some of its secrets. Barney saw that there were several concealed hunting knives and hunting bows within the cabin. Thankfully, the absent shepherd gave every indication of being an organised and resourceful fellow who was both capable and able to feed and fend for himself.

The storm continued to rage for the rest of that day and the whole of the following night until it blew itself out in the early hours of the following morning.

As the clouds parted and the sun peeked through, birds cautiously fluttered from cover; faint greetings were answered and then, within moments, there arose a raucous celebration of individual survival. When their feathers had dried and the birds were able to take flight they discovered that many of their usual roosts had been laid to waste. Uprooted trees and destroyed crops were scattered about as if a giant hand had toyed with them. Houses had been unroofed, and everything was sodden. Water and mud were everywhere.

The man on the horse had been forced to stop. After hobbling his mount, he had found scant shelter within a hedge that enclosed a large rectangular pen that enabled sheep to shelter from the piercing wind that sometimes roared across the plains. Once the worst of the storm had abated, the man arose, leapt on his horse and hauled the girl up in front of him before driving his heels into the horse's flanks, causing it to reluctantly set off at pace.

Both the man and the girl were drenched to the bone and cold. The girl's eyes were sad and puffy, as if she had been crying. From the stiffness of her movements, it appeared as though she was still affected by the massive bruise that had blossomed over her right shoulder and the grazes over a substantial portion of her body. Her teeth were chattering from the cold; even the heat of the man's body did nothing to warm her.

By the stream, the Captain and his enforcers had also risen. They were angry at having been consumed by the storm. Despite lacking food and rest, their first goal was to regroup so that they could search for the fugitives' trail.

In the hut, Barney woke first. Something was missing – the incessant pounding of the rain on the roof had ceased. He smiled to himself and looked over to where his companions were peacefully sleeping.

Barney tossed aside the blanket, padded over to the door and peered outside. The new day had brought sunlight with it. Gingerly, he touched his nose, which still troubled him. Grimacing, he realised that the skin surrounding his injured eye was still swollen. The skin was likely coloured yellow; however, he could now open his eye and it appeared that his sight had not been affected.

Barney stoked the fire, adding to it sodden wood he brought in from outside. It would burn to ensure that the warmth in the hut was not lost, but he hoped that the chimney would cope with the additional smoke it would create. Realising that when Shine and André awoke they would be hungry, he set about preparing the morning's meal.

The aromas generated from his cooking gradually spread throughout the cabin, stirring Shine and André's appetites. Over breakfast, they decided to wait for at least one whole day to give Bertrand the chance to catch up to them and also to give them the time to regain their strength. Barney was happy with the decision, especially when he checked on the Prince who still had not stirred. The only remedy he could think of was to provide him with undisturbed rest in the hope that the healing process could take root. He found himself wishing that Lucy was here with them. He truly believed that she had the necessary skills to help the Prince.

After they had finished their meal, Barney proposed that one of them should take watch outside, and he and André went outside to look for a suitable vantage point. They decided that the best place was on the rooftop, beside the chimney. From that position, the lookout could easily warn the others of the approach of any stranger by banging on the roof. The downside was that the lookout would be unable to see very far, as the hut was in a narrow, crevice-like valley situated between, on one side, the rocky cliff face of a mountain which rose almost vertically above their heads and, on the other, tall grassy hills whose shadows would fall across the hut until at least mid-morning. While the hut was hidden from view, there appeared to be nowhere close from which they could easily gain timely warning of the approach of unwelcome visitors.

For a time, Barney considered searching for a lookout location further down the path; however, being separated was not something that any of them wanted. Besides, there was limited opportunity for the watcher to relay information back to the cabin unless they were in sight of it.

The Captain, his offsider and his hounds had found a place to ford the stream, whereupon they were reunited with the rest of the party. Out of necessity the pace of their search had slowed. At most, they could only trot their horses, as the boggy mire of mud was slippery underfoot and there was no use rushing and risking their steeds, particularly when they hadn't found any tracks.

Several hours had passed before the Captain and his enforcers were back at the point where they had first headed downstream. Determinedly and methodically, they headed upstream, looking for any clue about where their quarry might be.

Out on the plains, the man urged his distressed horse on. The girl sat without speaking in front of him: the warmth of the apologetic sun played on her face, expelling her shivers but not her grief.

Another hour passed and the hounds had found nothing. The enforcers looked to their Captain and waited for his decision. It was obvious to them all that the storm had washed away any tracks.

"Zane, your family is from these parts – what's the quickest way through these mountains?" asked the Captain.

"Two passes. The main one is to the east – it is the only one that can take carts and wagons. All the traders use it. There is a smaller one to the west. You can travel through it on foot or with no more than two horses abreast. It can't take carts or wagons."

The Captain unrolled a sodden map. "Show me."

The eastern pass was clearly marked. Zane pointed out the location of the lesser-known one to their west. "If I was on foot, and I knew the area, I'd go west. Less chance of being seen and more difficult to be followed."

"We'll split up. McGuire, you lead those two to the eastern pass – as it's an established route, it will be easy for you to find. Zane and I'll take the pass to the west. My dogs will come with me, as you couldn't prevent them from making an unnecessary kill. Don't draw too much attention to yourselves. We are deep inside the Kingdom and far away from any assistance. Don't expect to be reinforced if you get into trouble."

The party heading east pressed their horses away from their fellows. Coincidentally, their direction of travel was roughly parallel to that taken by Barney's party. The Captain called the hounds and Zane to him and then spurred his horse to the west, towards the second and closer of the mountain passes.

As they moved off in an easterly direction the three men were confident that they would catch up with their target. Cresting a low rise, McGuire pointed out what looked to be a faint plume of smoke that was coming from the hills due south of them. Fire meant warmth and comfort from the after-effects of the storm, as well as food. The enforcers had not seen any other signs of life or any settlements in the area, and Zane had confirmed that there was no other pass through the mountain range, so they deduced that the source of the smoke was a farming homestead.

The Captain had given McGuire orders to search the pass; however, the chance of hot food and dry clothing was too much for them to ignore. McGuire decided that he would try to locate the source of the smoke.

McGuire turned and edged his horse towards the wisp of smoke. He focussed on it and noted that it appeared to be coming from the very base of one of the mountain peaks. Everywhere about him, the ravages of the storm were apparent. He passed a white tree stump that was surrounded by the disintegrated remains of a once-proud tree.

Eventually, McGuire came to what could be best described as a game trail, which was layered with branches and leaves that had been violently stripped from trees by the storm. The debris created a natural matting that masked the presence of the mud beneath it.

Every step McGuire's horse took breached the matting and sank into the boggy mire of mud that had not been washed away by the rain. More often than not, the mud swallowed the entire fetlock of each of his horse's legs as it squelched along. McGuire, understanding the horse's discomfort, belatedly questioned the wisdom of continuing up the trail. If his horse slipped and became lame he would miss the rendezvous with his companions. He was about to turn back when the sound of horse's hooves on firm rocky footing carried from his iron-shod hooves to McGuire's ears. As his horse had secured firmer footing McGuire decided to keep pressing forward – he could no longer feel the tension of his mount through his thighs.

McGuire had been prepared to find a farming homestead on the open plains. However, his path led him between two trees and then to a crevice that had been carved out of the rock through eons of erosion. He was corralled between the grand cliff face of the granite mountain to his right and the steep vistas of rolling hills to his left. The path gradually narrowed until no more than three-line-abreast horses would be able to pass through it. Looking up at the slither of sky above him, McGuire realised that he could no longer see the smoke. It was likely obscured by the trees, hills and rocky outcrops to the side of the path. The confined space made him feel uneasy; however, his curiosity got the better of his creeping doubts and, as the path appeared to be the only way forward, he continued to follow it. Water still ran down the majestic cliff face.

Back at the shepherd's hut, Barney had been replaced by Shine on the roof and he was dozing inside when there was an urgent thudding on the rooftop.

André seized his sword and Barney lurched forward and lifted his bow from where he had placed it upon the floor. He struggled to attach a bowstring to it while inwardly cursing his stupidity in not having it ready.

"You in there," called a voice from outside. "I need to speak with you."

Barney gave up struggling to restring his bow and signalled André to stay hidden to the side of the door. Resting his bow against the wall beside André, he reached for the door handle and, after again motioning to André to stay quiet, he pushed the latch aside.

Barney edged the door open and peered outside.

Outside, just in front of the veranda, he saw a man sitting on a horse. His sword rested in its scabbard. He was dressed in leather overlaid by a thick black cloak that was still obviously wet from the storm.

"How can I help you, sir?" enquired Barney.

"I am here as a representative of your King. I am searching for a party of four who may have passed this way last night."

Unusual choice of words, thought Barney, 'Your King', not 'our King' or even 'the King'.

"Last night the storm hid everything. We didn't see anyone at all," replied Barney.

"We? Who else is here with you?"

Barney bit his lip. Another stupid mistake. Rallying, he tried to make up for his error. Even though subterfuge was not something that came naturally to him, recent events were causing him to learn fast.

"My father is a shepherd in these parts. He was with me last night. He is off finding the sheep that were scattered by the storm."

"Your yards wouldn't hold many sheep. They look run down and disused."

"We are poor shepherds, sir."

McGuire's eyes bored into Barney, "So you've seen no one and the sheep that you tend were scattered by the storm. Yet your father doesn't need a spare pair of hands to help find them?"

"Sir, as you can see from my face, I took a fall. He went alone to see if he could find where they might have fled while I prepared a meal."

McGuire prodded his horse forward, "I'll be joining you inside to sample that meal- "

As he spoke, McGuire's hand slid down to the hilt of his sword.

Without warning Shine leapt from the rooftop, swinging her staff before her. Although surprised, the man was able to lurch to one side and successfully evade the full force of the staff.

André pushed Barney aside and lunged outside.

The horse, spooked by the sudden appearance of Shine and André coupled with the noise of the staff striking the enforcer's armour, reared onto his hind legs, snorting and screaming as he did so.

McGuire was already off balance. As the horse reared, he found that his still-wet thighs had no grip. The violence of the horse's action caused him to pull hard on the reins to try to control his own momentum. The horse was standing on two legs and all McGuire's strength was bearing down through the reins. The horse was unable to lower his head - he was in danger of overbalancing and falling backwards. His nostrils flared and he snorted and squealed in fright - he wanted, no he needed to run away, so with all of his desperate strength, he contorted himself, twisting his neck and arching his spine.

The ferocious movements of his mount were too much for McGuire to control. Just as he realised that his grip was not enough to protect himself from the gyrations of his horse, he found himself tumbling through the air.

Barney watched with mouth agape as the rider landed on his head. The full force of the rider's weight came to bear on the base of his neck as his head twisted beneath him. McGuire's neck broke. His body came to rest with limbs askew, as if a puppeteer had cut all the strings that had been supporting him.

In panic, the horse took flight. He turned on the spot and galloped back down the path with nostrils flaring, eyes wide in fright and stirrups and reins flapping in the air.

As the horse shot along the path, he rushed straight past a weary horse that was plodding towards the hut in the opposite direction. The rider of the second horse watched as his own mount flattened her ears in fright, but before she could stampede after the riderless horse, he reined her in, forcing her to stay put. Fortunately, the animal was so exhausted that she offered little resistance.

The girl stiffened against the man but said nothing. The man muttered something darkly under his breath and drew his sword before spurring his horse onwards.

Shine had landed awkwardly on her ankle and was being helped to the hut's veranda by André, and Barney was checking the enforcer. None of them noticed the laden horse as it came into sight of the hut.

The rider observed that the people in front of him were not moving with any urgency. He sheathed his sword before calling out to the three of them. Startled, Barney looked up, uncertain how to respond, but then he recognised the rider – Bertrand had returned.

Bertrand walked his horse over to where Shine was sitting on the narrow veranda nursing her ankle. After climbing down, he gently lifted Lucy from his horse.

With outstretched arms Lucy fell upon her sister. To Shine's shock, Lucy started sobbing: her chest heaved as she burrowed into Shine, tears flowed freely and Lucy moaned in anguish. The intensity of the grief spilling from Lucy almost overwhelmed Shine.

Shine glanced up at Bertrand with a puzzled expression on her face.

"I couldn't save them," sobbed Lucy over and over again.

As Barney and André came running over, Lucy's story came gushing from her at a million miles an hour.

"Ma and Da are dead. They were killed in front of me. Da was only trying to help me. They didn't have to –"

"What? Who?" interrupted Shine.

"The Duke's men found our camp. They had followed the tracks of some of our men who had stolen cattle for food. We had just butchered the cattle and were celebrating 'cos it was going to be the best meal the camp had prepared in ages. There were potatoes and mushrooms and –"

"Lucy! Focus! Please."

"Sorry. As I was saying, the men had just butchered the cattle and we were preparing the vegetables and fruits like a proper feast when there was a commotion on the edge of the camp. Cavalry – they had the Duke's colours – came rushing into the camp. We tried to run away from them, to escape them, but there were foot soldiers with bows shooting from the trees from the other side of the stream. Whichever way we ran, they cut us down.”

“You poor thing,” said Shine, trying to imagine the panic that must have been caused by the unexpected attack.

“We were in the centre of the camp and a group of us tried to surrender, but one of the cavalry kept crying out, ‘Death to thieves!’ We all ran to the far side of the camp away from the stream, looking for a way out. Ma was still sick and couldn’t move fast. A man on a horse ran her down because she was too slow and couldn’t keep up with the rest of us. Da wanted to go back to help her, but he couldn’t as he had me. It was my fault that Da didn’t save her. My fault that he wasn’t able to go to her. I tripped over and he stopped to help me up. I’m too clumsy –”

“Shhh. It’s ok. You’re safe now. It wasn’t your fault.”

For a while Lucy sobbed in her sister’s arms before she continued, “A group of around eight of us made it to the trees and split up. The arrows kept falling. Because I’m fast, Da and I managed to get ahead. Then one of the soldiers on horseback caught up with us. He swung his sword at me, Shine. At me! But Da pushed me aside and he got in the way. I killed him as well Shine. Da died because of me.”

Shine held Lucy tightly against her chest, tears welling in her own eyes, her ankle forgotten for the time being. Slowly, Shine rocked Lucy back and forth in her arms.

“Then the man jumped down from his horse and threw me to the ground. He was laughing at me. I kicked and bit him, but he was too strong. He was pinning me down and then suddenly he stopped moving and fell on me. I didn’t know what happened, but there was blood everywhere and then Bertrand had me. He pulled me out from under that man and put his hand over my mouth. I thought he was going to hurt me, so I bit his hand and screamed for help. He slapped me, Shine! He hurt me and then he bound my mouth and my hands so that I couldn't call out to Da. I wanted to go to Da, but Bertrand wouldn't even let me say goodbye. I hate him for that! He ignored me and just threw me on the soldier's horse like a sack of grain and we rode out of there. He must have killed three or four more of them before we broke free. He just kept riding. He nearly killed the horse trying to make it go faster and then he wouldn't even stop for the storm until the horse refused to go on-"

Once again, tears got the better of Lucy and she sobbed into her sister. Shine's own tears began to mingle with those of her sister.

As Shine tried to console Lucy, Barney and André looked away, respecting the sisters' grief. Tears of sympathy brimmed in their eyes. Bertrand turned to them. "The Prince?" he quietly queried.

"Alive," replied Barney.

Bertrand sighed. Then, steeling himself for the inevitable reaction, he said to Lucy, "The Prince will die soon if he doesn't receive medical care."

She stiffened and glared at Bertrand.

"So, you only saved me because you needed me? Why should I help him? I don't know him. You wouldn't even let me try to help my parents. Why is he more important than them?"

Quickly, Barney intervened.

"You're a healer, Lucy. You couldn't save your mother or your father because of events beyond your control. I couldn't save my mother or my father because they were killed by events beyond my control, but in there, Lucy, is a boy. That boy might be a prince and born to station, but he is still just a boy. The Healer from Marydale removed an arrow and stitched him up, but he hasn't stirred in days. We need you to help him. If you don't help him, then he will surely die. You have every right to refuse – in this you have total control – you, and you alone, need to determine his fate."

For what seemed an age, Lucy hung in her sister's arms with Barney's words playing over and over in her head. Suddenly she decided. Suppressing her emotions, she wiped her eyes with the back of her hands and stood up.

"Show me," she said with a steely determination that belied her emotional state. Suddenly and unexpectedly, Lucy had a purpose, and that purpose would, for the time being, act to drive some of her grief to the back of her mind.

Barney took Lucy's hand and led her into the hut. André wrapped his arms around Shine, lifted her in his arms and carried her inside. Bertrand felt forgotten and superfluous as he leaned on one of the posts that held up the roof over the veranda. He peered through tired eyes with a bemused expression on his face, as he wondered whether he should impose his presence on those inside the hut.

TWENTY-THREE

—◆—

Even once Lucy's eyes had adjusted to the dim light inside the hut, she could barely make out the Prince where he lay on a bed on the other side of the room. She squinted and then sniffed with displeasure at the stuffiness of the room and the stale smell of old cooking in the air.

The boy lay sweating on the bedding, his skin almost translucent white. One of his arms hung limply off the side of the bed. Lucy immediately felt for his heartbeat. It was extremely faint. She felt the Prince's brow and his chest. His skin was clammy. Then she inspected the half-closed wound on his back. Looking at Barney, she raised her eyebrows and gave him a look that reminded him of the contempt that his mother would direct his way when he had done something really, really stupid.

"Wound management Barney! Don't you know anything? Clean and dry, clean and dry, the basics of care and rest for a patient. The wound is infected, he has a fever and his heart is beating shallowly. Do you seriously think I can save him?" She stood with her head cocked and hands on her hips, as if she expected a fight.

Barney felt as though he were walking on eggshells and chose his words very carefully.

"I believe that you are the only one of us who might be able to save him. You are his only hope. We don't know what to do. Please try."

Barney's response tempered Lucy's mood. She sighed, paused and looked for a moment as if she would refuse, but by then, her brain had already betrayed her and was racing ahead, selecting remedies and discounting treatments. Finally, she settled on the course of action that she would take.

"You'll have to do everything I say. I have no time or patience for questions. Firstly, open the shutters. We need fresh clean air in here."

"We don't know how."

"I suggest you ask Bertrand. I expect he knows, and don't interrupt again! André, clean out the biggest pot that you can find. Make sure you scrub it clean. Then boil me fresh water in it! Barney, I'll need some herbs that should grow around here. Fetch Bertrand and I'll describe them to him. I then need you to sharpen and clean the smallest knives you can find. I'll have to remove the old stitches and some of the skin."

Lucy was right. Bertrand did know where the mechanisms to open the window shutters were and, luckily for him, he recognised the descriptions of wheatgrass, alfalfa and five or six other herbs that Lucy listed.

As he left, Bertrand enquired, "When will he be fit for travel?"

Lucy spun around and stamped her foot. She was tired and emotional and she laid her feelings bare, "If the Prince doesn't have assured rest and care for at least seven days, then don't bother getting the herbs; just dig a grave!"

Barney had never seen anyone as chastened as Bertrand was as he hastily left.

Once Bertrand had disappeared from her sight, Lucy interrupted Barney's knife sharpening as she needed him to assist her to turn the Prince completely over so that she could carefully examine his back. She pointed to the edges of the wound, which were bright red with pus-y green goo seeping from several places. Again, she remarked at his stupidity in not keeping the original dressing dry or asking the Healer for more of the poultice so that he could have spread it on the wound.

Barney tried to explain but Lucy raised her hand to stop him.

"I told you not to interrupt me. If you hadn't been so careless as to lose the backpack I gave you, then you would've had everything necessary to care for the Prince. I gave you specific instructions about the use of the antiseptics! Did you even listen to me?"

"I got dragged away from it--"

"Really! Is that your excuse? Blame someone or something else. You didn't think to hide the backpack so that you could return to it in the event of an emergency."

"But--"

"No buts! You carry him here through one of the worst storms that this county has ever seen and you don't even think to try to waterproof the wound."

"We didn't--"

"Have anything? Is that what you were going to say? My goodness, you poor thing. How silly of me. Your ears are open but they do not listen. Nature's garden would have provided. Bark from a tree or the largest of leaves bound tightly against the wound. Or how about a saddle bag or a hat or just about any piece of leather? Or splicing your precious quiver and binding that tightly in place--"

"We were being pursued--"

"So? You never had a rest break? Honestly, you took less care of him than you take care of yourself! You should take more care of yourself... and... and... you definitely shouldn't have allowed anyone to break your nose!"

Lucy was panting and her eyes were full of tears. As she stopped speaking, she hit him on his chest simultaneously with the sides of her fists, and then she stood there, less than an arm's length away from Barney, waiting for something. Barney didn't move. He was more confused than angry at the outburst.

The moment passed.

Catching sight of Shine smirking at them, Lucy spun to face her.

"And, as for you, dear sister, do you seriously think that it is appropriate or safe for you to leap from perfectly good rooftops? Do you think you can fly? He might be stupid and clumsy when it comes to caring for patients or avoiding having his nose broken, but at least he can still walk. You risked your life for no good reason. I can't fix a broken neck or a spine. As it goes, you're worse than him. Are you going to be guided by your very obvious brain impairment to do it again? If you are, then you can expect no sympathy or help from me."

Chastened, Shine looked away from Lucy's blazing eyes.

"I guess not," she mumbled.

"Don't you dare guess! You will or you won't."

"Sorry, sis. I won't do it again."

In the kitchen, André continued to scrub a pot, wishing himself invisible.

"Humph. Hurry with the knives, Barney! The Prince shouldn't be kept waiting any further."

André allowed himself to breathe a sigh of relief and went to fetch water for the newly cleaned and very shiny pot.

After Bertrand found the plants that Lucy needed, he brought them to the door and passed them to her. She snatched them from him without thanking him and immediately busied herself with the preparation of several different pastes and mixtures.

Once Lucy had cut away the stitches, removed some of the tissue and finished her initial dressing of the Prince's wounds she took the time to bind and splint Shine's foot. Then, after noticing the blisters on her sister's hands, she had all three of them stand in a line so that she could inspect, clean and then bind their hands. By the time she had finished, her wrath might have been spent, but their hands were still stinging from the lotion that she had spread on them.

When she returned to the Prince's side, Barney slipped outside to avoid any more of Lucy's stinging assessments of his behaviour.

Many hours later, as the sun set on another day, Lucy was satisfied that, for the moment, she had done all she could. She busied herself preparing the evening meal.

As they ate, Bertrand asked many questions about the pack of dogs that they had heard pursuing them. He had examined the body of the rider and found all the man's many knives and weapons. He expressed his concern that the man was too well armed to be a simple traveller. In Bertrand's opinion, the man was most likely one of their pursuers.

That night, after burying the body, Bertrand insisted that, apart from Lucy, they all take turns on watch further down the pass. He showed them a rocky ledge where they could watch without being seen and a short cut from the ledge back to the hut that would allow the lookout to warn those in the hut before any intruder was upon them.

Cautiously, after Barney came off his second watch, he approached Lucy who was at the Prince's side, placing a cold compress on his forehead.

"How's he doing?"

Conflict showed in Lucy's eyes, as if she didn't want to be the bearer of bad news, "I've tried everything, honestly, everything. I've even tried to combine a few treatments, but there's nothing Barney. There is no change. His breathing slows. His heartbeats are softer. Nothing I do appears to matter. Nothing I do appears to be working."

"Would you like to discuss what you've tried out loud? It might trigger a memory or an idea. I might not be able to suggest anything, but I can listen as long as you'd like. I'm sure you're helping him," he finished meekly.

Lucy gave him a warm smile.

"You think too much of my skills. The Healer had begun to teach me about what's needed in this situation, but

I've never had to put that knowledge into practice. His condition... is not good. It's right at the limit of my ability. I do know that if he deteriorates much further, I'll have no chance of bringing him back. His condition is just not stabilising..." Her voice trailed off.

"You brought me back."

Once again she gave him a warm smile, but this time it tinkered with her eyes, "Truth be told, I might have made the poultices and suggested the treatments, but it was Ma who stayed by your bedside most of the time. I'm beginning to understand why she did it. Once you start treating someone, you kinda make a promise to them to do your best. It's like making a promise to a friend. I couldn't stop now even if someone told me to. It's like I take and hold a piece of their lives in my own heart – they become part of me. I'm personally responsible now. Whatever the outcome, I know one thing for sure, I will write down all the remedies I use or discover so that someday they benefit all."

Barney hadn't realised that he had drawn closer to Lucy. He reached out and used his fingertips to brush away an errant strand of hair that was obscuring her downcast features, "Hey. You've got this."

Lucy lifted her face and her eyes captured his. Once again, Barney felt as though Lucy was searching for something. She gently shook her head, as her brow furrowed and tears welled in her eyes. Then, as he stood there looking at her, her features changed and Barney sensed her determination grow to meet the task before her: she visibly lifted, as if she were drawing strength from him.

"Death claimed my mother and my father – this time I will deny him."

Lucy turned back to her patient. For a while Barney watched silently until he moved away to leave the two of them alone. Before he lay down to sleep he looked back at Lucy and watched as she lay an ear to the Prince's chest – it was perhaps the most intimate thing that he had ever seen.

TWENTY-FOUR

Bertrand placed Shine on watch for lengthy periods to enable her to rest her ankle. While she looked out for any foe, Bertrand put Barney and André to work constructing a barricade. They used some of the furniture from inside the cabin, tree branches, thorn bushes (which scratched every conceivable part of their bodies as they tried to move them) and anything else that they could find.

Lucy took no turn on watch. Somehow she managed to stay awake tending her patient. It was a painfully slow process until the boy's colour began to return.

On the afternoon of the fourth day, the Prince's eyes opened to the sight of Lucy looking directly down at him. She had been in the midst of cleaning his face after attempting to administer more of her potions. He tried to speak, but only managed several unintelligible sounds before the effort became too much for him and he closed his eyes again. Lucy smiled and dabbed his brow as she watched her patient drift into a shallow sleep.

TWENTY-FIVE

The following morning the Prince awoke, frightened by his unfamiliar surroundings. He tried to rise, but Lucy laid her hand on his chest to prevent him from moving. The Prince remained awake long enough to be propped up, a position that was far better suited to him sipping water and it also allowed him to swallow more varieties of herbs to help his system recover.

It was mid-morning when the Prince woke again. This time he wanted answers as to where he was and who they were. Lucy summoned Barney and Shine. While they launched into a lengthy explanation of events, Lucy curled up in a ball on a nearby chair and surrendered to sleep. She didn't feel Barney come over to her and drape a blanket over her sleeping form before tucking it under her chin and covering her exposed ear, although she did smile in her sleep. Much as the Prince had needed sleep to recover, so, it seemed, did Lucy. With her patient now awake, the immediate danger to his health had passed. It was time for

Lucy to rest with the confidence of someone who knows that their skills would not be immediately required.

That night was a happier time. As the night wore on Barney couldn't continue to restrain his curiosity, "Why were you at the Baron's castle in the first place? My father didn't tell me that there would be a royal visit."

Lucy butted in, "Barney. Don't tax his energy."

"No. It's alright. I'm up for it. I was there because of one of the more pointless traditions of this Kingdom. I travel in secrecy so that I might 'learn about my Kingdom and its people'. The secrecy is to enable the Crown to disavow any of my 'adventures'. Officially, I am away serving our Kingdom by meeting with some emissaries. By not travelling under my title, I am not required to live up to it. My father and his father did the same thing. If my unofficial visit to the Baron had gone well, then I might have been fostered to the Baron for a period so that I might develop into a statesman and a warrior."

"What happened?"

"Barney..."

"Hard to say really. My uncle and the Baron have been squabbling for years. I don't know why he attacked, but when he did, he chose the southern approach to the Baron's castle as it's the least guarded. There are no fortifications between the Baron's castle and Marydale because the Northerners are meant to come from... well, the North."

His listeners nodded.

"We believe that advance units of my uncle's army infiltrated Landsend under the cover of darkness. Quite smart, really. There is always a large assembly of folk at the castle's gates first thing in the morning – you know the sort – the usual messengers, traders, emissaries, change of guard or common folk seeking to petition the Baron. The best of my uncle's men-at-arms simply waited amongst the other folk for the gates to open, but their intelligence was incomplete.

"The portcullis was raised, and the drawbridge lowered, but those with local knowledge paused while my uncle's soldiers stepped forward. You see, the Baron sends out regular early morning mounted patrols. They gallop around a bit, show the flag and practise. Keeps everyone happy, feeling that they were being protected."

The Prince took a draught of water, emptying the cup.

"Anyway, as I was saying, when the portcullis was raised and the drawbridge lowered those with regular business in the castle stood aside to allow the cavalry through; however, my uncle's men were too eager in moving forward to hold the doors open. It would have been over in moments if they had just kept calm. Well, they rushed straight into the path of the Baron's mounted cavalry just as the horses were spurred into a canter.

"The Baron managed to capture some of my uncle's men – they have since told us that they believed that they were betrayed and, as they were keyed for battle, they drew their weapons to fight the cavalry."

The Prince turned to Lucy.

"May I have another cup of water before I go on?"

"You needn't continue... you need your rest," Lucy said, as she went to fetch her patient some water.

But by now Bertrand was interested, "Go on."

Lucy pursed her lips.

"Well, they had the advantage of surprise, but there were men-at-arms waiting to enter to attend to their duties and the night watch was behind the cavalry as they were going to their homes. So, the Baron's forces had the weight of numbers. It got a bit dicey, but my uncle's men, despite the reinforcements that were pouring from the town, were beaten back from the entrance. Thereafter, the Duke's main force entered Landsend and the castle has been locked down in siege."

"But why not just stay inside and wait for the King?" prompted Bertrand.

"My advisers discovered that the Baron had been negligent in his duties. The castle was not stocked for a siege. It has been so long since the Northerners had attacked in force that the castle was ill-prepared. My advisers thought it best that I leave as they didn't want me to continue to be exposed to the war or, if my uncle was successful in breaching the walls, they didn't want me falling into the hands of his troops.

"It took a while, but my advisers scouted the walls and convinced the Baron to adopt their plans for an escape attempt. The Baron readied his cavalry in reserve, should assistance be required, but it appears that both plans failed, and we now find ourselves here, marooned in this... hut."

The Prince lapsed into silence and, despite their many unanswered questions, they all knew that now was not the time to ask them.

Finally, after more stories were shared long into the night and the watch was changed several times, it was time for them to clean up and fall asleep. They did so with satisfied smiles on their faces from the effects of their first 'normal' night together, which had passed in such gentle companionship.

CHAPTER

TWENTY-SIX

—— ✦ ——

Back on the grasslands, the Captain and Zane had returned, after their unsuccessful search of the western pass, to the stream where they had split from the other group. The Captain had decided that if the second party had found nothing, they would return to the Duke's army, as there were no tracks for his dogs to follow and the fugitives now had at least a five-day head start.

The land was drying out, lending itself to quicker passage, and they made good time as the Captain, his hounds and Zane began their search for the missing enforcers.

As they cantered through the landscape, the Captain spotted a saddled, riderless gelding ahead of them, eating grass. He looked up and whinnied in recognition and the dogs made no attempt to chase him. The horse watched the men approach but made no attempt to shy away. He had to be one of theirs.

Zane tied the horse's reins to his saddle and they moved on, keeping careful watch for the rest of their party. The Captain was left to wonder whether the horse had sprung free because of a riding accident or something far more sinister had occurred.

After an interminable hour had passed, the Captain was relieved to catch sight of two of his enforcers coming towards them. He was further relieved to see that they were not pushing their mounts as if they were being pursued. He stopped and waited for them.

"We rode most of the pass – no sign of them. We questioned the few that we came across, but they claimed that they hadn't seen or offered shelter to anyone," reported one of the enforcers.

The Captain paused a moment and gestured towards the riderless horse, "Did you get separated?"

"Aye. We saw some smoke from a homestead and McGuire went to investigate. Thought he might be able to rustle up some warm food. We was heading back that way now."

Irritated, the Captain nodded to himself in a silent admission of defeat. The boy had escaped him yet again. He could feel the tendrils of a dark mood reaching out from within him. He had never been able to curb his nature. He was on his own now – when his enforcers sensed his state of mind, they would jump at every command to prevent incurring the wrath of his displeasure – they would offer no counsel even if it meant going against their instincts. Hot food, a chance to rub the horses down and some sport for his dogs, out of sight to passersby, sounded like a very good idea.

"Show me," he said through gritted teeth.

One of his enforcers gestured back towards the mountains and urged his horse forward so that he might lead the way. The opportunity for provisions and sport with the occupants of a simple homestead were a much more attractive prospect than personally having to deal with the murderous mood that now gripped their Captain.

The hounds roved around their horses as they cantered on. Eventually they caught sight of three sets of hoof prints set into mud – two going one way and one the other. They slowed their mounts to a walk once they came to the pass between the mountain and the hills. There was no reason to rush.

The squad moved in single file without any attempt at stealth. Subconsciously, they each swept their hands over their clothing to ensure that there was nothing that would entangle the draw of their swords.

As the shadows cast by the afternoon sun caressed the hills and rocky outcrops above them, they came to the narrowest part of the path, which was directly below the lookout.

CHAPTER

TWENTY-SEVEN

——— ✦ ———

High above the path on the lookout's ledge Shine was sitting with her foot elevated while she daydreamed about decisions made and opportunities lost. The patterns made by the shadows as they played across the landscape served to further distract her as she wondered how fabric might capture the images. She found herself enjoying the solitude.

Shine's distraction was so complete that she did not realise that riders were beneath her until the baying of hounds seeped into her consciousness. They had caught her scent. She looked down, her reverie shattered. The riders frightened her, but it was the pack of dogs that sent a shiver down her spine.

As unobtrusively as possible, she rose to her feet. Although her ankle was much better, she still used her staff as a crutch.

Ordinarily, her movement in the deep shadows of the rock would not have attracted attention, but ordinarily, the men below would not have had hunting dogs. The pack caught sight of her movement. As one, they turned and pointed their bodies and snarled in Shine's direction.

The Captain looked up to see Shine hobbling towards a ridgeline. Too far for a bow, he thought. There was no way that the King's troops would be based in the narrow defile, but there was no point leaving witnesses to the theft of any stores, and he needed an outlet for his frustrations. He raised his arm. The dogs looked at him in anticipation. Palm down, he swung his arm towards the ground and nonchalantly commanded, "Kill!"

His instruction released the hounds and they leapt forward, scampering for sufficient purchase on the rocks so that they could climb to their target.

"Move on," the Captain called to his enforcers as he kicked his horse into a trot and drew his sword.

The Captain dismissed Shine's presence from his mind. His beloved dogs were better and more thorough at following his orders than most of the men under his command.

As Shine crested the grassy outcrop, she frantically waved her arms to attract the attention of the party in the hut below.

The Prince was seated in a chair on the veranda, while Lucy sang softly to herself as she prepared the evening meal inside the hut. André, who had been working on the barricade, caught sight of Shine before Barney and Bertrand did. Heedless of Bertrand's cries to remain at the barricade, André drew his sword and sprinted off to help Shine.

Bertrand and Barney seized their bows and positioned themselves behind the barricade.

Shine hobbled down the hill as fast as she could; however, her ungainly movement and the uneven ground caused her to trip and fall. The dogs behind her were in full flight and they had a singular purpose – to reach the girl and rip her apart.

For the first time, André heard the baying pack. He increased his speed. Lucy appeared in the doorway of the cabin and surveyed the scene as Shine struggled back to her feet. Lucy then withdrew out of sight.

As the Captain trotted around a narrow turn in the path, his horse shied, disturbed by the sudden appearance of the barricade. The hesitant sidestep by the horse saved the Captain's life. An arrow from Bertrand's bow flew through the air where the Captain had been only moments before. It struck the rock behind him, ricocheting harmlessly to the ground.

The Captain's men moved around him and, three abreast, they pressed their horses into a controlled gallop towards the barricade.

The man in the middle died as two arrows slammed into him.

"Dammit," hissed Bertrand, "Don't waste your shots. Call your targets. Left is mine."

Above them, the dogs had crested the hill and the lead animals were closing in on Shine, who was now standing. She turned to face them with staff in hand.

At the sight of the hounds, André accelerated. Once more Lucy appeared in the doorway of the shepherd's hut. She sighed and took a short leather strap and several round pebbles, the size of a small child's fist, from the pouch that now hung from her belt. Beside her the Prince went to rise – a curt direction from Lucy made him sit back down. Lucy stepped from the veranda.

As the horses sped towards them, Bertrand sighted his man and loosed an arrow. It caught him on the shoulder. His horse, feeling the enforcer's change in weight as he involuntarily leaned back in his saddle, stopped as she had been trained to do, but the enforcer didn't stop. He flew over the horse's head before punching a hole through the barrier. He came to rest at Barney's feet. His passing had dislodged a table and as it fell to the ground it left a gap in the defence.

As Zane spurred his horse to leap clear through the gap, an arrow from Bertrand's bow buried itself in his hip. The Captain followed closely behind Zane. It was his intent to close on the archers before they could fire again. The Captain caught sight of Barney and sneered as he felt his pent-up rage build inside him. Nothing would stop him from destroying the boy. Not even the pint-sized man before him who had cast his bow aside and even now was daring to draw his blade.

The hounds reached Shine. The lead animal was immediately beaten savagely by the staff that she wielded, breaking its back. The second had several ribs broken and the third died by André's sword. One of the remaining dogs then leapt, sinking its teeth into Shine's left leg before André struck it down. The jaws of another latched onto the end of Shine's staff and leaned back, pulling with all of its weight and strength. The pack smelt fear and blood: this was what they had been bred for; what they had been trained to do. Shine was the target of choice. They had been ordered to take her. Moving in, they sought to hold André at bay while they overwhelmed Shine.

The situation was desperate. The hounds closed in and cramped André's ability to swing his sword. André lashed out with his foot, viciously kicking a hound that was seeking to flank Shine. He threw his sword at another to distract it. Reaching to his sides, he drew two long knives from their sheaths. Yelling and screaming to attract the pack's attention, he ran at them, stabbing and slashing at anything with fur as he went.

Zane's horse caught Barney on his shoulder, spinning him to the ground and knocking the bow from his hands.

The Captain urged Zane to attack Barney while he charged at Bertrand – his closest threat. Bertrand met the Captain's sword with steel of his own. The angry and bitter clash of blades sang out.

Zane gained control of his horse and swerved to get behind Barney. As he raised his sword to strike, he heard a whirring noise followed by a sharp pain on his shoulder. Startled, he looked about, only to see a small girl reloading a sling before she started to swirl it at waist height.

Zane's momentary distraction was enough for Barney. Launching himself from the ground he seized Zane around his waist and pulled him from his horse. As they hit the ground they rolled away from each other, stood, and drew their knives.

André was tiring. He was covered with blood, some his own and some from the dogs. Countless bite marks and scratches covered his skin. The sheer weight, size and speed of the pack was wearing him down and his reactions were slowing. Shine was doing her best, but because of her injuries, it was unlikely that her best would be good enough.

A dog to the right of Shine suddenly yelped in pain and shied away. Then a dog to Shine's left also yelped in pain and cowered away. Suddenly, Shine had room to swing her staff and use it as a spear. More of the pack lost its focus due to the unexpected and silent force.

Turning her head, Shine caught sight of Lucy as yet another rock was flung: this time towards a dog that had circled behind André.

"What?" called out Lucy with an impish grin on her face. "You think all those ducks and birds I brought to the dinner table died of natural causes?"

Shine shook her head and half-smiled. Refocusing her attention, she unleashed her remaining strength, swinging her staff with lethal precision. Stepping forward, she positioned herself at André's side, guarding his back.

The Captain had Bertrand's measure. From his greater height on his steed, he could swing down and drive Bertrand back. He would enjoy this kill.

The Captain drove his sword down hard, slicing its tip across Bertrand's upper body, forcing Bertrand to drop his sword and fall to his knees.

Undetected by Lucy, the Prince, kitchen knife in hand, shuffled to assist Bertrand. He was barely well enough to walk unassisted.

The Captain noticed the advancing figure and immediately recognised the King's son from the Duke's description. His vengeance would have to wait, as the reward for bringing the boy to the Duke far outweighed the significance of his revenge against the farmer's boy.

To his right, Zane, despite his injured hip, strove to kill the damn boy whose size and speed were his only advantages. The boy was nipping in to cut and stab. Above him, his beloved dogs were dying at the hands of two foe. For the moment, the Captain held the upper hand, but if his dogs were defeated, then he would no longer have the numerical advantage.

The Captain drove his spurs into the flanks of his horse. The horse surged forward and knocked Bertrand to the ground. When Bertrand struggled to rise, the Captain swung his sword down hard. The dulled blade struck Bertrand on his shoulder and the Captain had the satisfaction of feeling the blade jar against bone. Once again the Captain mercilessly spurred his horse, but this time he urged it onwards towards the Prince.

Lucy sought to retrieve another stone from her pouch but found it to be empty.

The Captain reached the Prince. He leaned down from his saddle, brushed aside the kitchen knife and grasped the Prince by his hair. With one swift movement, he hauled the Prince onto the pommel of his saddle.

By now Bertrand had staggered back to his feet and was holding his sword with his uninjured arm.

"Zane! Clear my path. I have the Prince!"

Startled, Zane disengaged from Barney and lurched towards Bertrand who, despite his injuries, batted away Zane's sword, sidestepped to his left and thrust his own sword into Zane all the way to its hilt.

The Captain drove his spurs into his horse. All he had to do was clear the barrier.

From the corner of his eye, he saw the farm boy loose an arrow from his bow. It flew at point-blank range into the Captain, punching through the leather cladding and into his body, whereupon it continued to burrow into his side. Blood poured from the Captain's wound. The arrow had penetrated so far that only half of the arrow remained visible. Blood rose to the Captain's lips as pain lanced through him. He lurched to the side, pulling on the reins. This motion caused the horse to spin on the spot which, in turn, caused the Captain to grip tighter to his saddle. This effort at self-preservation loosened his grip on the Prince, who slid free.

The horse now faced towards the remaining hounds. She erupted into a gallop, with the Captain just hanging on. As the horse swept past Shine and André, the pack turned and followed its master. The horse had her head and swept on.

Of them all, only Lucy hadn't suffered a wound. Stuffing her sling carefully back into her pouch she brushed her front with her hands and assessed the scene. The Prince, although winded and shaken, had little outward signs of any traumatic injury so, for the time being, she dismissed him as needing immediate treatment.

Lucy catalogued the probable injuries in her mind. She decided to help Shine and André first. She would have to clean and dress the wounds quickly, as there was no telling what infections the bites might cause. When she got to them, she found that André had collapsed on the ground from his exertions. It was difficult to determine how many times and how seriously he had been bitten, but he brushed her away and pointed to Shine. Lucy could see fresh blood pouring down Shine's leg.

As Lucy approached Shine, she passed a dog whose spine had been crushed. It bared its teeth, and despite its pain, it growled at her. Lucy rested her hand on its head before gently pushing it to the ground: and then she crouched down and softly slit its throat. Suddenly there was silence.

TWENTY-EIGHT

—◆—

Although Lucy believed that she had catalogued the injuries in order of priority and severity she quickly discovered that her list was incorrect. The worst injury was to Bertrand's shoulder. Fortunately, it seemed that there would be no permanent damage but, in stitching and dressing the wound, Lucy found that Bertrand's back was thick with scars that could only have been caused by a whip having flayed Bertrand's flesh, permanently disfiguring it. Bertrand refused to comment about the origin or motives behind the punishment and Lucy was left to wonder once more about who Bertrand actually was.

As she finished applying first aid to all of their injuries, some of which would leave permanent reminders of the brief but vicious encounter, Lucy saw one of the four horses that were busy cropping grass turn her head, ears raised, towards the barricade. A man had appeared. His bow was held but not drawn. An arrow was notched in place.

Barney started towards his bow.

"Hold, Barney," said Bertrand, "These men are known to me and besides, that one arrived over half an hour ago... if he wanted you dead, you already would be."

"Men?"

"Yes, Barney, there are three of them now. I sent for them before you had escaped the town, but as usual... they're late." Bertrand directed his voice at the man, "Put your bow away. These folk are with me. You took your time."

The man nodded in Bertrand's direction, shouldered his bow, and raised his hand palm up to shoulder height. Two other men, one crouched at the scene of Shine's fight and the other to their left, rose from their vantage points.

"Well, if you'd sent for us sooner and perhaps if you'd had the power to hold off that wee storm, we would have arrived a little earlier. What happened here?"

"No time for telling. I have the Prince. I need two of you to remount. Follow those tracks, and be quick about it. A red-haired fellow escaped on horseback. Track him down and ensure that he doesn't return this way. He is injured, but he has hunting dogs with him, so stay downwind. Dean, you stay. I need you to gather the horses and hobble them and make sure that they don't escape. We will need them on the morrow. We also have to clean up this mess and bury the bodies. You'll be standing guard tonight."

The men nodded. They started their tasks immediately, barely acknowledging Barney and his friends.

"Who are you?" Lucy asked Bertrand.

"You know who I am. These are friends of mine, so they are friends of yours," replied Bertrand in a manner that didn't welcome further discussion.

Barney drew his bow and pointed an arrow at Bertrand.

"What do you want with the Prince?"

All the new arrivals stopped, frozen to the spot.

"Stop!" cried the Prince. "I believe that I know of these men. I believe they are loyal to my father."

"I wasn't asking you."

Bertrand slowly turned to face Barney. "I am the King's man and so are these men."

Stretching his good arm out wide, he stood still within a body length of Barney. "Kill me or don't. I leave that to you, but think on two things. Firstly, I could have dealt with you and your friends many times over and then turned the Prince over to the Duke, but I did not. Secondly, why would I be ordering two of my friends to seek out the leader of the men that attacked us? Why didn't I just allow them to overpower you all when they first arrived?"

Barney continued to sight the arrow as he thought through the events of the last few days. What Bertrand had said was true, but the situation had him on edge. He didn't feel in control; he didn't feel as if logic had any place in what was happening to him. He desperately wanted to roll his father's pawn between his fingers. Sweat beaded his brow.

He felt a warm hand come to rest on his forearm. It was Lucy.

"Barney, he has absolutely no reason to lie. Put down your bow and go tend the horses."

Barney could feel Lucy's large almond eyes pleading with him in raw silence. He paused and took a deep breath, held it for several seconds and then emptied his lungs of air. He felt like he was drowning in events and that his life was heading along a path where he simply could not foresee what would happen.

As he breathed out, he gently let the tension out of the bowstring. Without a word, he handed the bow and the arrow to Lucy and trudged towards the horses. His hand went to his pocket where he found his pawn.

Dean raised his eyebrows in an unspoken query directed at Bertrand who shook his head. They all let Barney go without further comment.

By nightfall, Dean, with some assistance from André, had managed to bury all the bodies. Afterwards, it was a welcome relief to find that Lucy had cooked a somewhat eclectic feast using every available ingredient. Even she did not know how it would taste. Fresh mushrooms and fruits sat beside a stew made from boiled meat, salted fish and anything else she could find.

After capturing the horses, removing their saddles and wiping off their sweat and trail dust with cloth and straw, Barney brushed their coats before preparing their feed. The repetitive movements in caring for the horses had helped him clear his head and somewhat reduced his misgivings.

When Barney entered the hut, he nodded at Bertrand, who came to him with hand extended. Barney shook it after only a slight hesitation. He understood that at this point in time, he and the others were reliant on Bertrand, but looking into Bertrand's eyes, he wondered if he could ever trust this man or ever regard him as a friend.

Following Bertrand, he went to the table to eat. Outside, Dean had been watching Barney while fingering his bow. After Barney had entered the cabin without commotion and had accepted Bertrand's greeting, Dean shrugged his shoulders and accepted the fact that this would be a very long night for him. He pulled some jerky from his cloak before heading off towards the lookout where he would stand watch, a task he had undertaken so many times before.

TWENTY-NINE

N ow that they had horses and didn't have to walk, Lucy was able to be persuaded that they could travel the next morning. However, she would not be rushed, and she flared again into anger at the suggestion that there was no time to check the dressing of their wounds. It was well after mid-morning by the time they set off.

They had six horses and seven people, so Barney insisted that the Prince rode in front of him. Dean stayed another hour at the hut to place himself between any enemy and the small party.

The pass that the companions followed from the hut was so narrow that their legs on one side brushed the cliff face and, on the other side, shrubs and thorny bushes pulled at their clothing. The path was clearly not frequently used. At Barney's insistence, Bertrand begrudgingly explained that they were, in fact, travelling on a relatively unknown poachers' path; in the circumstances it was probably the safest route that they could take to enter the Kingdom's heartland.

Late afternoon found them at the mouth of the path that opened into a plain of cultivated beauty. The fields held many varieties of crops and the sheer expanse of land without a horizon packed with snow-capped mountains took their collective breath away. They crossed through the first of the fields and came to a road which they turned to follow.

The final ride turned out to be wholly uneventful. Slowly, over several days, they travelled deeper and deeper into the heart of the Kingdom. At first, they encountered standalone homesteads until, eventually, they came to small villages where they sourced fresh food from roadside vendors. For the most part, they were avoided or ignored as they were, at first blush, mainly a party of travelling youth.

Are you certain?"

"The message is brief sire, but it is from Bertrand himself."

"Alive? And no longer in the Baron's castle? How?"

"It appears so. We do not know how, sire: we have little to go on."

"I told that damn fool not to risk the life of my son by making a rescue attempt!"

"Yes sire. We have no details of events."

"Could this be a trap? Could my brother be playing us for fools?"

"We do not know, sire. I have our best ready to ride at your orders."

"I will go myself."

"That is unwise, sire. If this is a trap, then both yourself and your successor will be in the same place at the same time. It will be like flies to a honeypot. One strike and all is finished.”

“He is much more to me than my 'successor'. He is my son. I. Will. Go.”

“But sire...”

“Detrix, I do not require your further counsel on the matter. I have questions for Bertrand. Do not tell my wife what is afoot – she is troubled enough already. You will go to my army – I will be delayed by one day. I will ride in the guise of William. It has been a long time since I have used him to be amongst my people – let us hope that I have not forgotten how to play the part. We will need a ruse to ensure that those who watch me do not suspect that I have left here – make it so!”

“It will be as you say.”

“Do we know where they are headed?”

“Bertrand has a preference to stay at the Boar's Head before entering the Citadel.”

“So be it. We ride at once.”

THIRTY-ONE

———— ✦ ————

On the final night before they reached their destination, Bertrand directed them to an inn where he paid for lodgings for the six of them. The next day's ride would bring them to the King's Citadel where the Prince would once again be under the protection of his father.

Sitting at a long table, eating food and drinking watered wine, the companions enjoyed the singing of a bard who walked through the inn playing his lyre while singing his songs. Barney, André, Shine and Lucy discussed their future once they had delivered the Prince back to the King while, at the adjoining tables, their fellow patrons discussed rumours of a major battle to the north.

None of the companions had any family to return to. They were all orphans in an adult world. There would be no returning to the farm for Lucy and Shine, as their parents' death meant the land would revert to the Baron who would choose its next tenants – a child was not permitted to inherit a farm.

André had no desire to return to being a merchant or, for that matter, to become a farmer. He wanted to explore and experience the sights and sounds of the Kingdom.

Barney was confused. His parents were dead and he had no skill that would enable him to become an apprentice; he had no desire to be on his own, yet he had given his word to André that after delivering the Prince to the King, he would be on his way, never to be seen again.

On into the night they talked, attempting to unravel the tangled web of their futures while the bard played on and the number of patrons in the inn diminished. The Prince and Bertrand were silent for the most part, leaving the four companions to hold court.

Finally, Lucy rose from the table declaring, "Barney, you gave your word to André. I want no part of it. It is my view that we are family now and families stick together. André, release Barney from his oath, as I tell you now that if I had been there, I would have prevented him from ever making such a silly statement. I will ignore his promise to you. I will see him again and I suspect that you will see me again, so let us stop this foolishness. Whatever will be, will be, but we will face it together and woe betide anyone who gets in our way. To bed!"

André said nothing as they left the table. They retired to a dormitory of some twelve beds, four of which were occupied by the bard and three other recumbent men. Quietly slipping into the room, the companions went to lie on their beds.

"So, Bertrand, what do you bring me?"

"Is it wise to discuss this now with you in that guise?"

The bard swung his feet over the side of his bed to the floor as Barney and his friends stopped in their tracks. None of the other three men feigned sleep any longer. They had sprung to their feet with a long blade in each hand.

Barney and André pushed the Prince and the girls behind them, each taking a dagger from their belts.

"Traitor," hissed Barney at Bertrand.

"Hold, Barney... it is not as you think."

Barney and André crouched low, gauging the men as one of them circled to the door, blocking their exit.

"Humorous. You think that you children could take down three members of the Black Watch?" asked the bard.

Barney looked at André, who shrugged back at him. Neither of them had heard of the Black Watch. This wasn't unusual, as the existence of the secret organisation, although rumoured, was known by very few people in the Kingdom.

The Prince pushed André and Barney aside, "Good evening, Father."

The bard ignored him completely.

"Will you vouch for them?" he asked Bertrand.

Barney had heard the term before and he understood the serious nature of the question. The bard was basically asking Bertrand to stake his life on the companions' past and future loyalty and conduct.

"Lucy is a physician by heart. Barney a leader and thinker. Shine will do anything to protect those around her. André is a lovesick puppy who's fairly good with a sword and can take instruction, and he has the muscle necessary to enforce the will of the party," Bertrand said in reply.

"They are witnesses to my brother's attempt on the life of my son."

"M'lord, they have done nothing wrong. They saved your son."

"I ask again: do you vouch for them?"

"I do."

"So be it. Counsel them to silence, split them up and send them far from here. If you are wrong, then your life–"

"Not wise, m'lord."

"You tread on dangerous ground to interrupt and disagree with me. You have much explaining to do and your status is not enough to protect you from my displeasure."

Bertrand bowed low, "No offence intended, m'lord, but they have talents and are reliable. I counsel you to give them to me."

The bard paused and regarded Bertrand. For Bertrand to ask such a thing and vouch for them meant that Bertrand was not only impressed by the group before him but was willing to stake his life on the fact that the group would enhance the Black Watch, which the King's great-grandfather had set up so many years ago. Bertrand was asking for the four companions to be commissioned into the Black Watch.

"So be it. I rely on your judgement and will hold you accountable. Counsel them to secrecy. My kingdom is divided enough as it is."

"We will test them, m'lord. Should they fail or disappoint, then we shall deal with them."

"Father, I insist that you hear me."

"Be quiet."

The Prince stepped in front of his father, "No, I shall not be quiet. These four saved my life, so I owe them my life and it is a heavy burden."

"The time for blood debts and blood feuds was over a long time ago. I have decreed it!"

"I regard it not as a blood debt. I regard it as a duty to repay a service that was rendered without hope or desire for reward. You heard them tonight. They spoke nothing about receiving a reward in gold from you. They spoke of family and loyalty. Are these not attributes that should be rewarded?"

The King hesitated, a hardened glint returning to his eye, "So how would you explain to the court why these four strangers should be given titles, land or rewards in gold?"

"You misunderstand me, Father."

The room was consumed by the sudden tension of observers to a family disagreement between two of the most powerful people in the Kingdom. Everyone wanted to remove themselves from the room but none could.

Raising his eyebrows, perhaps in surprise but more likely in irritation, the King responded, "The Black Watch's sole duty is to act as my ears and eyes and to protect me and mine. You have heard Bertrand commit to finding a place for them, yet you object to this. I personally ensure that the needs of every member of the Black Watch are met. I will remind you but once that my will is law and you are bound to obey! You have one chance to convince me to reconsider. Your thoughts – and be quick about it."

"I offer them my friendship and protection and in return they become mine. You have the Black Watch whose loyalty to you is without question. I want my own guard. I want a group that I can be myself with. I want these four to receive training to be my eyes, my ears and my protectors. Will you allow me to do this?"

The King, despite himself, was impressed. He had sent away a young boy to learn something of his Kingdom and had not expected his rather selfish son to mature in thought so rapidly. Perhaps there was more to him than the spoilt only child of an overprotective mother. For the first time in his life, it appeared that his son felt a degree of loyalty to someone other than himself.

He turned and acknowledged the group of four, "Lower your weapons. You stand in the presence of your King. You have heard my son. What say you?"

The four looked at each other, bewildered by the course of events. The Prince was offering them an opportunity to stay together and to gain purpose. They had no ties to anyone or anything and there was no apparent downside to the arrangement.

"You refuse to answer your King?"

Barney sheathed his knife and turned to the Prince and knelt on one knee before him, "I freely offer you my service."

Lucy and Shine followed suit. Only André remained standing.

Barney looked up at André, "Please forgive me. Please join us," he begged.

André closed his eyes. Barney had already pledged himself to the Prince. If he joined in, then it would be he and not Barney who had created the circumstances whereby Barney's oath to him could not be honoured. Barney's conscience would be clear. He should walk away, but that would mean leaving Shine, as she had also already bound herself to the Prince. He could not bear to think that he might lose Shine. He was a prisoner of his feelings, and he knew it. Slowly he took a knee beside Shine, "I too freely offer you my service."

Shine gently took hold of André's hand.

The companions had pledged their allegiance to the Prince, not to the King, and by doing so they had removed themselves from the King's direct influence.

"I accept," said the Prince. "And I release Bertrand from being responsible for their conduct. I alone will be responsible for them."

The King's face was expressionless. He understood the gravitas of what had played out before him. It was a completely unintended outcome, but he could think of no way to undo what had been done. He had placed four of his subjects within the sole authority of his son and it was to his son that they had sworn allegiance. The Prince had publicly disavowed Bertrand as being responsible for the group's actions. He could now only hold the Prince responsible for their conduct. He had allowed the creation of a small group within his Kingdom who were outside of his direct control and his son's life could be held forfeit for their behaviour. It made him uneasy, but he could not remove the potential threat to his son without ordering the Prince to take back his statement and, if he did that, he would forever undermine his son, even if such an order was given only in the presence of his most loyal men.

"Bertrand, I ride with my army to meet with my brother in the morning. My son will be escorted to his mother. You are required to attend me on the morrow at dawn – you have much to explain. My army is due west of here. Are you well enough to travel?"

"Yes, m'lord, I have received the best of care and am assured a swift recovery."

"These four are not to come."

"It will be as you say."

"We will speak of the skills that are needed to be taught to these... what will you call them, my son?"

The wound on the Prince's back itched in reminder. That arrow had delivered him into the hands of his companions, it marked the start of his time with them, but it was not the reason for them being there. He frowned as his thoughts sifted through Lucy's rambling tales to the very beginning. Unwittingly, the arrow that had killed Barney's father had set off a chain of events that had led to the formation of this group of friends who stood before him.

"I shall refer to them as the Black Arrows, Father."

"Very well. Bertrand, let the Black Watch know that the Guild of the Black Arrows has on this night been formed. Their duty and loyalty lie with the Prince of the Kingdom. The Black Watch is to train them and assist them as if they were part of the Watch. The Watch is not to interfere unless they turn against my orders, against my son, or endanger my kingdom, and their number is not to expand without my express consent. Do you all understand?"

"Yes, sire," was the reply.

And thus it was that the Guild of Black Arrows was formed.

EPILOGUE

U nfortunately, the members of the Black Watch who Bertrand sent after the Captain didn't manage to catch up with him. Although severely wounded, he was still able to warn the Duke that the Prince had escaped.

The Duke knew that his chance to gain the throne through the capture or death of the Prince had passed and he immediately acted by lifting the siege on the Baron's castle and withdrawing his army towards his territories.

Bertrand later admitted to Barney that he and the other members of the Black Watch had been ordered by the King not to intervene in the siege. The King had given these orders because he did not know whether the Duke was aware of the Prince's presence, and he believed that his son was safe, as the castle had been built to withstand a siege from armies of far greater numbers than those of the Duke. Despite his orders not to enter Landsend, Bertrand had led Barney and Shine there so that he might gain knowledge of the Duke's forces through his own observations and through whatever intelligence they could glean. He would have used that knowledge if the Black Watch had been authorised to make a rescue attempt.

The King, together with Bertrand, who was posing as his senior military member of the King's entourage, rode out the morning after the formation of the Black Arrows. They rode with three thousand cavalry to intercept the Duke. They caught up with the retreating army at a place called Cal Mead on the border of the Duke's County.

In private conference with his brother, the Duke denied knowing that the Prince was in the Baron's castle when he attacked. He insisted that he had attacked in response to a series of raids that had been sponsored by the Baron.

The King berated the Duke and demanded that reparations be paid.

Bertrand explained to Barney that the King could not prove that the Duke knew that the Prince was in the castle when he attacked; the Prince's location was, after all, a state secret. The King could not risk outright war with his brother and his brother's followers unless he could prove that the Duke's attack was an attempt on the life of his only child. Despite being pressed, the Duke carefully maintained his position that his actions were based on a feud arising from a territorial dispute.

The Duke negotiated from a position premised on his knowledge that the King's main armies were engaged on the Kingdom's outposts. To decisively crush the Duke, and to prevent the country from falling into civil war, the King would have to recall his armies, which would risk the King's hold over the outer reaches of his Kingdom.

On the other hand, the King knew that the Duke had to be careful, as he could ill afford to risk his men by overtly attacking his brother. Such an attack would enable the King to call upon all the six counties to provide him with the troops necessary to put down the uprising. The King also knew that if he was struck down and his son still lived, the Duke would, once again, be passed over in the line of succession by the Prince.

Once the parties realised that it was a stalemate, the terms of an agreement were struck, the terms of which were satisfactory to neither of them.

Riding to the Baron, the King delivered the news of the negotiated settlement. When the Baron took issue with the settlement's terms, the King pointed out that his only child had been seriously and needlessly wounded when he tried to escape a castle whose stores should have been enough to withstand a six-month siege. The castle's defences and stores had, in the King's view, clearly not been kept in accordance with pre-existing decrees.

In a heated discussion, the King accused the Baron of being ill-prepared and negligent in his duties and threatened to remove the Baron from his position unless he accepted the terms of the settlement with the Duke. The King insisted that the Baron take Bertrand as the King's representative to assist in the rebuilding of Landsend and to ensure that the castle's defences were brought up to the required standard.

Reluctantly the Baron agreed, but not before, at Bertrand's suggestion, the King impressed on the Baron that there was to be no retribution taken against the Healer or any of the Healer's family or against any of the people of Marydale who had been forced into the Duke's employ.

When he left the Baron's castle, the King knew that notwithstanding the agreement, the Duke's ambitions were still in play. He had acted to prevent civil war, but he knew it was only a matter of time before he would have to take care of his brother. The King also knew that those Council members who would prefer the rule of his brother would be emboldened by the action taken by the Duke and the simmering dispute between the brothers. Sides would be taken and posturing for position could be expected to reach a fever pitch.

The Black Arrows left the Boar's Head with the Prince to travel to his private wing of the King's castle at the same time as the King and Bertrand left to meet with the Duke. Once they arrived at the Citadel, the Black Arrows were to be placed amongst the palace's general retainers and given the duties of personal servants to the Prince. Any official duties would leave them with sufficient time to meet with members of the Black Watch who would develop their skills so that they could safeguard and preserve the Prince's life.

At the Citadel, the Black Arrows, in their sworn duty to protect their Prince, needed to hone lifelong skills through practice and patience. Their skills would be needed for many years to come.